MW01137572

Black Friday

Published by Jan Stryvant
Copyright 2017 Jan Stryvant

#53682D

ISBN-13: 978-1979790710
ISBN-10: 197979071X

Jan Stryvant Books:

The Valens Legacy

Shadow

Black Friday

Sean looked both ways as he started across the street, not that there was much traffic during the day here at the University of Nevada, Reno campus this late in the day. But it always paid to be careful; some of the freshmen came from serious cow towns to the north and never seemed to look where they were going.

Mid-terms had just finished, and he was pretty happy with his grades this semester; he'd finally gotten the hang of this whole 'college' thing, so what if it had taken him nearly three years! True, it wasn't UNLV. Going to the university's Las Vegas campus had really sounded like a lot more fun than being in Reno, but in some ways maybe this was better. Reno had a lot less traffic, and…

"Hey! What the hell are you doing!" he yelled, as suddenly a car pulled out from the curb, the engine revving as some stupid freshman farm moron blasted out from the curb, straight at him!

Diving between two parked cars in front of him, Sean heard the squeal of brakes and laughing from the car's open window.

"Better pay attention, couch jockey!"

Getting to his feet, Sean glared at Dean Hoskins, the backup quarterback for the Wolf Pack.

"Least I'm not a camper!" Sean shot back. He didn't like Dean; the guy was all ego, and word was he'd been quite the high school ball player. But apparently that wasn't good enough to cinch the starting position here at UNR, and that failure had led to him finding unfortunate targets to release his frustration on.

Sean had come to his attention at a LAN party at one of the local frats when he'd fragged Dean fifteen times in a row. The only thing that had stopped Dean from beating the crap out of him had been the football coach's rather strict policy on his players getting into fights. But it still hadn't stopped the harassment.

"Better watch your mouth, Sean, or one of these days, you and I are gonna have a little dance!"

Grumbling, Sean turned his back on his harasser and continued walking across campus towards his room. Maybe he should start carrying that can of pepper spray Sampson had given him. While he wasn't exactly afraid of Dean, Sean really wasn't all that interested in getting beat up, either. Sure, he could hold his own in most fights, but most of the fights he'd been in as a kid hadn't been with a college athlete in perfect physical condition.

Turning a corner around one of the buildings on the edge of campus, Sean's attention was suddenly brought back to the present as someone grabbed him from behind.

"Dean!" He yelped and, dropping his book bag, he thrust an elbow back, hitting somebody who grunted in a much deeper voice than Dean's.

A van screeched to a halt in front of him, the side door sliding open, as a man with his face covered jumped out and ran to help the guy Sean was now struggling with. When a hand came over his mouth as he started to yell, he bit down hard, enjoying the curse of pain from behind him. The guy was distracted enough for Sean to move to his right and slam his hand back into the man's crotch. Grabbing a handful of balls through the fabric of a pair of slacks, Sean squeezed hard and ducked his head, butting it into the stomach of the man running at him as the other man let go.

"Use the taser, you fool!" someone shouted, and almost instantly it felt like something bit Sean in the side, then his whole body spasmed in pain as he heard a loud clicking sound.

Falling to the ground, he hit his head on something and could only see stars, then darkness as a hood was thrown over his head and he was bodily hoisted up and thrown into the back of the van, the door slamming closed. From the way his body was rolling around on the floor, he could only assume they were rocketing off rather quickly.

Gathering his wits a moment, Sean kicked out with his legs; luck was with him, as his feet connected with somebody. There was a brief flash of pain as he heard the clicking noise of the taser again, but it was only for a moment. He heard someone yelling and cursing, then the van started to rock back and forth for a few moments before coming to a rather abrupt stop with a loud crashing noise.

Flying forward, he tried to tuck himself instinctively into a ball, but he slammed into something hard and passed out.

Sean came to slowly to the sound of gunfire. In the tight enclosure of the van, it was painfully loud. Grabbing for the hood over his head, he gasped in pain, his right arm lit up in agony. Using his left, he ripped the hood off and, looking around, it was complete and utter mayhem. He was covered in blood, and from the bone sticking out of his forearm, it was clear that a lot of it was his.

The van was a complete wreck, the windshield was gone, and from the blood and pieces of flesh on the broken, jagged edges, he suspected someone had gone through it. There was now a telephone pole where the passenger's seat used to be. The driver, who was either dead or unconscious, was slumped over the steering wheel, still belted into the seat.

The door on the side of the van was missing; it was just gone. The bright light of the afternoon sun was streaming into the van, which was full of dust and smoke.

There was another shot, then a loud scream of incredible pain. Turning to look, Sean saw that both of the rear doors had been ripped open, as they were both hanging from one hinge now. There was a dead body on the floor; just the body, there was no head on it.

He heard another gunshot and a loud roaring noise, and he looked over at... at what, he wasn't quite sure. He blinked and shook his head. There was a man, the one who'd jumped out of the van, if he was remembering the clothes right. He wasn't wearing a mask now, it was missing. He had a gun in one hand, some big shiny automatic – maybe a Desert Eagle? Living in Reno, he'd become rather familiar with guns.

But that wasn't the part that was strange; it was what the man was shooting at.

A lion.

He was shooting a lion.

But this lion didn't look like any lion Sean had ever seen before, and again, living in Reno, he'd seen quite a few. No, this lion was huge. Well wait, weren't all lions huge?

It hit him, it was a lion-man, and just as the kidnapper fired another shot, the lion-man finally grabbed the arm that was holding the gun, and with a sickening wet sound, he ripped it off.

Just like that.

He *ripped it off.*

The guy holding the gun fell back screaming, a rather high-pitched and pitiful sound, as he clutched at the fountain of blood coming out of, well, where his arm had once been. It was almost Pythonesque in the absurdity of it. You couldn't *really* rip a man's arm off, could you?

"Sean!" the lion growled, and Sean turned his attention back towards the lion-man. Yeah, it really was a lion-man, and he was looking at him. Sean blinked and tried to figure out just what the hell was going on, but for some reason, things were having trouble focusing. Something wet was running down his face, and he kept wiping at it with his left hand.

"Yeah?" Sean mumbled and looked around him.

"We have to go, *now!*"

"Umm, okay," Sean said and, scrambling towards the open side door, he fell out of the van onto the ground as his legs refused to cooperate. He inhaled sharply in pain as he hit the ground, his broken arm lighting up with fire again as he hit, and his right leg hurt as well. Looking down, he could see it was also bleeding through a fairly large gash.

"I'll carry you," the lion-man said and, picking him up with a loud grunt, he slung Sean over his shoulder.

Things were spinning; Sean could only figure that he'd passed out for a moment, and he was having trouble focusing on anything. He remembered then, he was bleeding. Right, he'd been in an accident. He needed to stop the bleeding. Bleeding was one of those things they taught you in the first aid class to deal with first, right?

At that point he was laid down on his back and, looking up, there was Sampson. Sampson was his next-door neighbor, or rather, his Mom's next-door neighbor. Sean had moved out last year. He was a maintenance worker or something at the casino where his Mom dealt blackjack, and an old family friend who'd once worked for his dad.

"Sampson?" he said, blinking. "What are you doing here?"

"Listen," Sampson grunted, and Sean noticed he was covered in blood, and from the way it was flowing, Sampson had been shot. Several times.

For some reason, that woke Sean from his daze.

"You've been shot!" Sean exclaimed in shock, his own pain momentarily forgotten.

"Yeah, that last bastard had silver bullets in his gun," Sampson growled. "I don't have much time, Sean. I'm dying. I promised your father I'd protect you. Guess I failed."

"Wait, what? My father?"

"They're after you, Sean. I don't know why; maybe your father left something behind for you, and they're afraid you'll find it and use it."

"Who's after me? What are you talking about?" Sean babbled. Sampson thought his father had left something behind? The only thing his father had left them had been a million dollars of debt!

"They'll be watching the hospitals, not that I'll live long enough to get you to one," Sampson gasped. "So I guess there's only one thing left to do. I'm sorry, Sean. I'd hoped you'd have a normal life.

"Guess that's over now."

And with that, Sampson grabbed Sean's broken arm and bit it, right over the wound.

Sean screamed, but it came out more as a gasp, and along with the pain from the bite, there came a cold burning sensation that spread through his body with an intensity Sean had never felt before as he passed out once more.

Just Another Day

Sean woke up slowly; mornings were never his strong point. Stretching, he opened his eyes and looked around his apartment.

As usual, the place was a mess; the window was also open, which wasn't too big a deal, considering he lived on the third floor. Sitting up in bed, he looked at the alarm clock. Eight AM. For the first time in a long time, he'd beaten the alarm. Getting out of bed, he looked down at himself in surprise. He was naked.

Why the hell had he gone to bed nude? Was he out of clean underwear again?

Grabbing the old watch he'd been given for his eighteenth birthday off the nightstand, he stared at it. It was Saturday. That was right. Yesterday was Friday. He'd left school on the way back to his apartment, and then……..

And then…what?

Looking down at himself, he didn't see any cuts or bruises, in fact he seemed to have lost some weight. Not that he was exactly fat, but with the last few years of eating poorly and sitting on his ass all day, he'd started to develop a bit of a spare tire. The rest of him also looked a bit more, well, *buff*.

"Have I really not been paying attention to myself that badly?" Sean muttered as he set the watch back on the nightstand and stood up to look at himself. He needed to hit the shower. He was smelly, even a bit dirty. But just what the hell had he gotten up to last night? He didn't do drugs, well, not much really, just the occasional joint or something, if someone else offered it. Same for drinking. As a college kid on a scholarship with a butt-load of financial aid and student loans, he really couldn't afford all that much.

Squinting a bit as he concentrated, he remembered walking out of the engineering building, then Dean being an asshole, again. *One of these days he was going to have to put that guy in his place...*

Sean stopped again. Where the hell had that thought come from? Keep your head down, avoid confrontations, get the degree, and get out of school. That's what his Mom had always told him. The only place he ever stood up to people was in online games or when role-playing at the weekly D&D session with his old friends from high school.

Walking over to the mirror, Sean looked at himself. He looked, well, more or less the same. How often do you really look at yourself in the mirror anyway? You just take it for granted after a while. But everything looked okay. He needed to shave, and he needed to wash, but otherwise?

Shaking his head, he grabbed his robe and towel, wrapped the towel around him, and headed off for the common shower he shared with the others on this floor.

He padded down to the bathroom; no one was in the shower, but this was a Saturday, so everyone else was probably just sleeping in.

"Oh, damn," a female voice said from behind him as he opened the door to the shower.

"Huh?" he said and turned around; Roxy was standing in her doorway wearing just an oversized t-shirt, looking at him.

"I was hoping to be first today!" Roxy pouted.

Sean had to smile. Roxy was the only girl living on the floor; she was a few inches shorter than him, sleek and slender, and cute as hell. She was on the track team; her specialty apparently was the hundred-yard dash. Looking at her standing there in nothing more than a very long t-shirt brought some rather impure thoughts to Sean's mind.

"I'll be quick; aren't I always?" Sean chuckled.

"Well, I'd hardly be in a position to know," Roxy teased back, then she suddenly looked him up and down with a rather frank appraisal. "You been working out, Sean?"

"Umm, yeah," was all he could think to say as he tried not to blush. Roxy had *never* looked at him like *that* before. Then again, not many girls did.

Hurrying into the shower, he closed the door behind him and put those thoughts out of his mind.

Roxy stood there in the doorway, staring at the closed door. She could smell it, he absolutely stunk of it. Lion. Sean smelled of lion. Had he met up with a lion-were last night? She didn't think he swung that way; he always struck her as more interested in women than other men.

Sneaking over to his door, she opened it and peeked inside. The place was a mess; she sighed at that, there was a pile of rags under the window. He was worse than her brothers!

The scent of lion was strong in the room, but how? If Sean had had someone up in the room last night, she would have heard it, hell her hearing was good enough that she could hear it when he jerked off; their rooms were right next to each other, and in these old converted houses, there wasn't much in the way of sound insulation.

She smelled the blood then. Looking down the hallway towards the shower, she heard the water come on, so she carefully snuck into the room. The smell was coming from the pile of rags under the open window. Looking back and forth around the room, making sure there weren't any hidden threats, she slowly walked up to it and, dropping carefully to her knees, she leaned over and gave the pile a sniff.

Blood, lots of blood, at least that of three different people. There was an older male lion's scent, very strong, but it wasn't the scent she'd gotten from Sean.

Roxy's eyes widened. Sean had been bitten! That had to be it!

This could be bad; there weren't supposed to be any lions around here. Werelions weren't common; they were one of the least common of all the were-races. Roxy had heard all the stories about them, though. They were strong, they were aggressive, and they were very territorial.

And they never, *ever*, converted humans! Either this was some kind of rogue male passing through, or something very bad was going on.

Sneaking back out of Sean's room and carefully closing the door behind her, she went back to her room. Closing her own door, she leaned back against it and blew out a breath she hadn't realized she'd been holding.

Sean was a nice guy, pretty much harmless, and obviously focused on his schoolwork – and video games, when he wasn't studying. She'd heard him mention that his Mom dealt blackjack at one of the larger casinos in town, and his father had died in some sort of industrial accident many years ago. Sean had been sketchy on that; Roxy figured it was none of her business, so she hadn't asked more.

Shaking her head, she hoped she was wrong, that maybe it was just that his scent mixed with that of the other male's was tricking her nose. Because while lions tended to be good, when they went bad, they went very bad, and for those who were bit and not born of the blood...she shook her head again. With no one around to teach him, the odds of his beast getting the upper hand were too strong to ignore.

She'd wait until he was done in the shower, then she'd go in and smell it herself. If she could still smell lion after he washed, there'd be no doubt about it, someone had bitten Sean.

When Sean left the shower, he was a little surprised at how quickly Roxy had rushed past him to go inside. Going back to his room, he dug out some clean clothes. He'd have to do laundry tomorrow morning; he was out of underwear after all.

Pulling on a clean pair of jeans and a t-shirt, he went over, sat at his desk, and looked around for his cell phone. It took him a minute to find it; it had ended up under his book bag, which looked like it had been dropped on the ground, as it had dirt sticking to it.

Opening his phone, which had gotten some brown, dried crap on the back of it, he started to look through his messages to see if he could puzzle out just where the hell he'd been last night.

There was a text from Chad, asking if he was coming over to watch some anime with him, Alex, Steve and Steve's girlfriend, Terri.

There was a second text from Chad three hours later asking where he was?

Alex had also sent one, with the same question.

Looking through his logs, he hadn't sent out any texts, nor gotten or made any phone calls. Sticking his phone in his pocket, he grabbed his socks and sneakers. He'd just have to go and retrace his steps.

After he stopped at the store and got himself some new sneakers, he realized, looking at his shoes. They were seriously torn up; the fronts had been ripped open, and they were both stained with something.

Shaking his head, he threw them in the trash and putting his boots on he left his room, taking the trash out and heading down to the bus station. Sneakers first, then he'd see about tracing his steps.

Roxy showered quickly; the scent of lion had still been in the shower when she'd come in. There was no doubt in her mind now, someone had bitten Sean. Who would do such a thing and how it had happened would have to wait. She'd have to confront him about it, and quickly, before he got settled into it and posed a threat.

But just how do you have that conversation with a guy you barely knew? Oh, she knew Sean thought she was pretty, she'd caught him checking her out more than once. But he probably figured she was out of his league. And until now, she'd definitely been just that, though not for the reason he'd have guessed.

Getting back to her room, she noticed he'd already gone out. That wasn't good. Sitting down, she grabbed her phone and looked to see if she had his number. She knew she'd never asked for it, she hadn't wanted to encourage him after all, but maybe she'd gotten it anyway?

"Damn," she swore softly. She didn't have it, and she had no idea if anyone she knew might. She'd just have to go down to campus and see if she could find him.

Getting dressed quickly, she left a note on his door with her number, asking him to call her, then grabbed her track bag to make it look like she was going to practice, and left.

The Worm Turns

Sean was walking on campus, retracing his steps from the Engineering building yesterday. He'd found the note Roxy had left on his door when he'd gone back to his room to drop off his boots and put on his new sneakers. It was in his pocket right now, actually. He'd never had a girl give him her number before, especially not one as cute as Roxy! He'd seen the kind of guys she'd dated before, even that one girlfriend of hers that he suspected might be a little more than a 'friend'. The guys were all a lot more athletic than he'd ever been. If he'd known that losing a few pounds could get him a shot at a girl like her, maybe he'd have taken his mom's advice about diet and exercise a bit more seriously.

But it was only right that she be interested in him now.

"What?" He stopped and shook his head. Where the hell had *that* thought come from?

Maybe instead of trying to find out what had happened to him yesterday, he should go check himself into the hospital. Maybe he'd gotten drugged with one of those 'date rape' drugs everyone was always talking about! They'd all been told that they messed with your memory and could cause mood swings.

Yeah, that was an idea.

Looking both ways, he started across the street, when a car abruptly peeled out from the curb. Looking over at it, Sean sighed. It was Dean again, pulling the same damn trick he'd pulled yesterday. Only this time, there were a bunch of his football buddies standing around watching.

For the first time, ever, Sean took a moment to look at their faces. A couple of them obviously thought it was funny, but most of the others were almost grimacing at what was happening.

His pride doesn't approve, he embarrasses them!

Sean didn't have time to blink, much less consider the strange thought. He simply jumped up in the air as the car screeched to a halt, the expression on Dean's face one of shock when he didn't move out of the way.

Landing on the hood of Dean's bright red Camaro, however, turned that look into one of pure rage as the hood scoop collapsed under Sean's weight.

Sean couldn't help but smile, and he jumped again, coming down hard on it a second time, denting the hood further with his weight.

Dean opened the door and jumped out of the car, screaming at him.

"My car! What the hell did you do to my car, you fucking couch potato! I'll kill you for this!"

Sean looked down at him, and for the first time in his life, he felt angry. Mad. Upset. *How dare this little fucking peon, whose own people didn't even like, threaten* him*! It was time to teach this little shit-stain a lesson!*

Stepping off the hood of the car, Sean looked at Dean, and for the first time he noticed that Dean wasn't any taller than he was, there was nothing special about him. He was just a boy. A very *ill-mannered* boy.

"Blow me," Sean said, staring him down.

"Why, I'll…" Dean said and, drawing back his arm, Sean could tell Dean was going to punch him.

"Dean! NO! DON'T!" his teammates started to yell.

Dean hesitated a moment.

"That's right, Dean," Sean growled softly, showing all the contempt he felt, "walk away before you get hurt!"

Dean struck, hitting him in the jaw, turning his head slightly.

Sean was surprised. Oh, it stung a little, but it really didn't hurt all that much. Dean was looking rather shocked as Sean suddenly grabbed his arm with one hand, his face with the other, and slammed Dean down over the hood of his car on his back.

"Any last words?" Sean snarled as he started to bang the back of Dean's head into the wrecked hood.

"Dude! Stop!" One of the team members was there, yelling at him.

Sean looked up at him, *how dare he interrupt?*

"Whoa! Take it easy, Man!" the guy said, holding his hands up and backing off. Sean recognized him; he was one of the team's linebackers, and he was backing off!

Sean's mind caught up with events suddenly. What the hell was he doing? He had Dean pinned to the hood of his car, and for all his struggles, Dean was unable to push him off, and a man who was five inches taller and probably a hundred pounds heavier was *backing away* from him?

"Sean!"

Sean whipped his head around. It was Roxy; she was in her running shorts and top. Obviously she'd been running; he could smell the sweat on her from here, and it smelled *good.*

"Let him go, Sean. He's not worth it."

Sean looked down at Dean. No, he wasn't worth it! What the hell had gotten into him!

Letting Dean go, he turned and started to walk over towards Roxy. Now *she* was worth his time, definitely worth it.

"Son of a…" he heard Dean swearing behind him. He just ignored it. "Let me go!"

"Dean! He was going to kill you, Man. Didn't you see his eyes? Leave it, or I'll go tell the coach, you understand?"

"Hi," Sean said, coming up to Roxy, all his anger melting away as he smiled at her, and tried not to feel too embarrassed. Yeah, Dean had deserved that, but why did he feel like the kid who'd just gotten caught with his hand in the cookie jar?

"I got your number," he continued, pulling the slip of paper out of his pocket and trying not to fumble it.

Roxy looked him up and down and couldn't help but smile. A moment ago, he'd been about to beat Dean into a coma, and now here he was looking all guilty and shy about getting caught in the act.

"So, why didn't you call me?" she asked, still smiling.

"Umm, well," Sean blushed and started to rub the hair on the top of his head, even more embarrassed. "Something sort of happened last night, and I umm."

"Yes?" Roxy asked and moved closer, looking up into his eyes as she moved into his personal space, almost pressing up against him.

"Well, I was trying to…" Sean noticed just how close she was to him, and how she was looking up into his eyes.

Kiss her! Came the unbidden thought.

What? And get slapped and lose her? he thought to himself, as he suddenly found himself fighting urges he'd never known existed in his body before.

"Let's go back to my place," Roxy said, grabbing his arm. She could see the conflict raging behind his eyes. His beast was starting to come out.

"Are you sure?" Sean asked, because he was totally unsure of himself right now; he knew if he got her alone, well, he was sure to get himself in trouble!

"Yes," Roxy said, dropping her voice to a more sultry timber, "I'm very sure."

Sean smiled down at her and, straightening up, he offered to take her bag with his free hand, then proudly walked her back to their apartments.

"So, what happened last night?" Roxy asked him as they strolled along.

"Umm, Welllll," Sean hesitated.

"You can tell me, Sean," Roxy said in that low, sultry voice. He'd never heard it before, and it was doing things to him. Nice things, pleasant things.

"I, I don't remember," he admitted, shaking his head.

"Nothing?" Roxy asked, glancing over at him with her head tilted to the side.

"No," Sean sighed and shook his head, "I remember Dean playing that trick on me yesterday," he growled as he said that, then stopped, embarrassed. Since when did he growl?

"So, I thought I'd come down here and retrace my steps. See if I could remember what happened." Sean looked at her with obvious worry in his eyes. "I wasn't drugged, was I?"

"Drugged?" Roxy asked.

"Well, you know how they talk about those 'Date Rape' drugs, they make you forget, they mess with your mind, you don't think…" he asked and looked down at her.

Roxy shook her head and chuckled. "No, Sean. You weren't drugged. You weren't drugged at all."

"Were you there?" he asked, suddenly suspicious.

"Nope, I have no idea what you went through, but I do know what *happened* to you."

"Really? What?"

"Let's wait until we get back to my place, okay?" Roxy said in that sultry voice and smiled as she lightly hip-checked him as they walked.

Sean grinned and nodded. He wasn't stupid.

The moment the door closed behind them, Sean pulled Roxy up against him. Wrapping his arms around her, he looked down at her, and kissed her.

It was wonderful. Sean may not have been the most experienced man when it came to women; honestly, he'd never gotten past first base with any of the girls he'd been with before. But then, none had ever tasted this good on his lips before.

"Don't you want..." Roxy started when he came up for air.

"Shhh, that can wait," Sean said and, ducking his head down, he kissed her again. Something inside was telling him to press on, to take her, that she wouldn't refuse him, she wouldn't say no.

"But I'm all sweaty and..."

"You smell wonderful." He sighed and stuck his nose in her long tawny blonde hair, taking a deep sniff, then rubbed his face in it. She just smelled so *good*.

Roxy sighed and smiled. Gone was the shy gamer nerd who lived down the hallway; in his place was a much more confident animal that knew what it wanted, and damned if her own beast wasn't responding! A lion. She'd never done it with a werelion before, of course she'd mostly stuck to her own kind, most did. Though she'd experimented with others; they all did, lycanthropes were a lot more laid back about sex than most humans.

But there was always something just a bit intoxicating about the biggest of the big cats.

"This will be a lot more comfortable on my bed," she whispered back huskily, and immediately found herself swept up off her feet as he carried her over to her bed and carefully laid her down on it.

He started with her sneakers, unlacing them and taking them off, then her socks. Pulling his shirt off, he started to kiss her legs and rub his head against her ankles and legs as he moved up the bare skin, getting her scent all over him as he rubbed his own into her.

When he got to her shorts, he just ripped them off of her, along with her panties, and she could tell that he hadn't even noticed he'd done it, so wrapped up in the moment, so much under his beast's control.

She quickly pulled her own shirt and sports bra off before those got ruined as well. But it was hard to be upset. She'd never had anyone rip her clothes off before, and her own beast had grabbed on to his hair and was steering him between her legs now, drenching him with her essence.

Sean couldn't believe what was happening to him. He had Roxy under him, naked, as he teased her with his lips and his tongue, his hands gripping at that tight little ass like a drowning man grabbing at a rope. She was delicious, and from the way her hands were pushing him down while her hips were grinding up, he could tell she was appreciating his efforts.

When she suddenly cried out in pleasure and shivered beneath him, he licked his lips and continued up her body, licking, tasting, and rubbing his face against her.

When he got to her lips, he kissed her, long and luxuriously, savoring the taste of her. He felt her fingers undoing his pants, pulling down his zipper and pushing his jeans down as she reached inside them, wrapping her fingers around his length, caressing him.

"I've never..." he whispered in her ear.

"I want you," Roxy replied and slowly guided him to her.

Sean couldn't believe it, the feelings, the sensation, the heat, the all-engulfing feeling as he slid into her depths. Any reservations he might have had disappeared as she wrapped her arms and legs around him and started to grind her body back against his.

He started off slowly, he didn't want to hurt her after all, but from the way her heels kicked his back and she started to get vocal beneath him, he quickly picked up speed and force. It wasn't long before he was panting above her, sweat dripping off his body onto hers below, and it all just overwhelmed him completely. How long it lasted he wasn't sure, but when he hit his peak and shuddered through his own ecstasy, he was pleased to hear her cries answering his as she shivered beneath him.

Roxy caught her breath as Sean collapsed on top of her, his arms wrapped around her taking some of the weight off. For a young man who'd just lost his virginity, he'd been pretty good. When she'd seen him about to kill Dean, she'd figured she'd just lure him back to her place with the unspoken offer of a little fun, then figure out how to tell him what had happened and offer to teach him about his new aspect.

But now? She smiled, and wondered if it was just because he'd been a virgin and she'd deflowered the nerd next-door, or if there was something about lions she couldn't resist? Then again, he'd always been nice and friendly enough to her; she'd just never considered him, because relationships between mundanes and lycanthropes never worked out.

Sean raised his head up and, looking down into her eyes, he kissed her. "Can we do that again?" he teased.

Roxy laughed. "Of course we can, and," she dropped her voice back down to that sultry tone, "we *will*.

"But first, wouldn't you like to know what happened to you?"

Roxy giggled as he blushed.

"Um, yeah, that would be nice too," Sean admitted.

"Okay, but first, how about we roll onto our sides? As much as I like being under a big strong man, you are a little bit heavy."

She smiled as he rolled off her onto his side, pulling her along, of course. Propping her head up on one hand, she smiled down at him.

"You know, there really isn't any easy way to say this, because you're not going to believe it until I prove it to you, so I might as well just say it."

"That doesn't sound good," Sean said a little worriedly.

"You got bit by a werelion, and he infected you. You're now a werelion."

Roxy watched as he simply stared at her for a moment.

"You're not laughing," Sean finally said after a minute of just staring at her.

"It's not a joke, Sean. Suddenly your body is ripped, and it'll continue to get more muscular over the next few weeks as your body adjusts. You bedded me without the slightest hesitation, though for the last two years the only thing you've done is stare at my ass when you thought I wasn't looking.

"You were going to beat Dean to death…....."

Sean blushed at that.

"And it doesn't even occur to you to wonder why you're suddenly stronger than him, faster than him, and why Miles backed off so quickly when you stared him down, though he's way bigger and stronger than you? Or at least he *used* to be stronger than you; now, who knows?"

Sean stopped and thought about it. Yeah, a lot of strange things had been happening lately. Not the least of which was, he was lying naked, in bed, with Roxy, stroking her hip slowly after having sex with her. But something about her words rang true.

"A werelion?" Sean asked.

Roxy nodded. "Yes. How you got bit by one, and why he decided to infect you..." she shrugged her shoulders, and Sean couldn't help but be distracted by her breasts as she did so.

"Hold on there, tiger!" She laughed and pushed him back as he'd been starting to go after this latest distraction.

"Don't you mean 'lion'?" he teased.

Roxy grinned again. "Try to stay on the subject for at least a little while, Sean. That's your beast distracting you."

"My 'beast'?"

She nodded. "Every lycanthrope, that is, every were-creature, has a beast inside them, their animal aspect. It's what allows us to change. When we become our beast, the beast takes the forefront of our minds while we sit in the back and advise them."

Sean looked puzzled for a moment. "And here I thought I was going crazy, because I've been having strange thoughts, like someone else was in my head."

"That's your beast. Lions tend to be dominant, strong, very focused on order and their prides; they're sort of the organizers and rule-makers of the cat kingdom."

"But," Sean looked confused, "where did he come from? Was he like, injected into me or something?"

Roxy shrugged again. "No one really knows. Some think it's something born of your own ego, given shape by the particular strain of lycan you become, but I honestly couldn't tell you. The thing you need to understand is that he's there, he isn't going away, and you need to accept that, to accept this new part of you, or you'll have problems."

Sean followed all of that, and considered it for a moment.

"So how do you know...wait a moment," he said, "you said 'allows *us* to change'!" He looked her over, carefully now. "Are you a werelion too?"

"No, werelions are rare; well, at least around here they are; I'm a werecheetah."

Sean opened his mouth, closed it, then opened it again; there was one way to find out if she was telling the truth or just pulling his leg.

"Prove it!"

Roxy smiled at him, and just like that, there was a cheetah-girl lying where Roxy had been. If he hadn't had his hand on her hip, if he hadn't felt the sudden surge of, something, if he wasn't now stroking a hip covered in short fur, he'd think he was dreaming. But the strangest part of all was that, rather than being scared, that new 'part' of him was suddenly getting very excited.

"I, I think this is going to take a little while to get used to," Sean said, looking her over. She was bigger now, at least as tall as he was, and there was a lot more muscle on her frame than before. She still had the blonde hair, and while her face now had fur and a muzzle, it still looked a little like her.

"This is my hybrid form," she told him, her voice slightly changed. "Where both my beast and I co-exist in equal parts."

"How do I do that?" Sean wondered out loud.

He got whacked by her tail then. She had a tail! And she laughed at the expression on his face.

"First you have to master your lion form. Once you've achieved harmony with your lion, and your lion with you, then you can try it."

She shifted back then, and once again, it was just him and a beautiful naked woman.

"You look pretty hot like that, you know."

Roxy grinned. "Of course I do! But my beast is *very* interested in your beast, and well, right now I'm afraid you might end up a lot worse for wear if I stayed like that."

"I thought cheetahs and lions didn't get along?" Sean said, trying to remember some of those nature shows he'd seen.

"While we share some traits with our native species, we're still half human. There's a certain commonality amongst all of us lycans," *and*, she finished quietly to herself, *some cheetahs can be terribly subby when presented with a nice big dominant lion.*

And apparently one Roxy Channing was suddenly feeling very subby. The idea of not just having a lion, but raising him up to be the kind of male she liked, was quickly becoming rather attractive, and not just because her beast was pushing for it.

Sean sighed and shook his head. Looking over at her, he just shrugged and pulled her closer.

"You seem to be taking this rather well," Roxy purred as he started to run his hands up and down her body.

"Right now I'm in bed with a lovely woman who wants me," Sean said, smiling slowly. "I think that kind of overrides any other worries or problems I might have. I'm sure I'll freak out afterwards."

"That's your beast talking." Roxy chuckled.

"Well, at least he's got good taste and good sense!"

Sean kissed her again, and decided to work his way south this time to investigate that rather inviting bosom of hers. Stopping halfway, he looked up at her with a puzzled expression on his face.

"Does this mean I'm going to want to change into a lion at every full moon?"

Roxy grinned and pushed his head back down. "No, that's wolves."

A muffled "oh" was his reply.

"Cats like to shift during the new moon, when it's darkest."

Sean shut up then, and decided to concentrate on better things, namely Roxy's chest.

Jump Right In

"I'm hungry." Sean sighed as he snuggled up against Roxy, discovering she fit rather nicely against him.

"I know, I can hear your stomach!" she chuckled.

"Well, let's hit the shower and go get some food?"

"That sounds like an idea," Roxy nodded, "go grab your towel."

"Umm," Sean said, looking at her, "you want to shower together?"

She laughed. "I don't see why not. I look the same wet as I do dry."

"I'm not so sure about that," Sean replied, laughing as well. "We might end up in there until midnight."

"Don't worry, once the hot water runs out, so will we!"

Sean had to admit that showering with a woman was fun. Though sex in the shower sounded better than it actually was; water had a tendency to wash away natural lubrication.

They returned to her room and got dressed; Sean was getting hungry enough that thoughts of fooling around were now taking second place.

"Let's stop by your room first," she suggested.

Sean shrugged. "Okay, but why?"

"I want to look at the clothing you had on yesterday, that's all."

Sean nodded and unlocked his door as she locked hers.

"Sorry about the mess," he said, a little embarrassed.

"Eh, typical problem of the male condition," she said and went over to the pile of clothes directly under his still open window.

"Don't you ever close that?" she asked.

Sean shrugged. "We're on the third floor, not like anyone can really jump that high."

"I wouldn't be too sure about that," Roxy said and pointed to eight parallel claw marks on the outside window ledge.

Sean gulped. "I did that?"

Roxy nodded. "Yup." She picked up the small pile of clothes on the ground by the window; a pair of pants, mostly shredded; a shirt, mostly shredded; a pair of underwear, mostly shredded; and a pair of socks that were just missing the toes. "And you did this, too."

"Well that explains my sneakers." Sean sighed.

Roxy nodded. "Yeah, shifting is hell on clothes, part of why I wear shorts and stretchy fabric if I think I might have to shift."

"So, you're saying I shifted then?" Sean asked, looking at his clothes as Roxy started to sniff at them. "What are you doing, anyway?"

"Trying to identify whose blood this is."

Sean turned pale. "Those are blood stains?"

"Yup." She turned and looked at him. "You live in Reno and you've never seen bloodstains before?"

"Wellll, not ones that big! There must be enough blood there to…" Sean trailed off as he thought about it.

"Kill a man?" Roxy asked.

Sean nodded dumbly.

"Actually, I suspect it was at least two, and there's a lot of blood from the werelion that bit you as well."

"Do you, do you think I did it?"

"Considering that a lot of this blood is yours?" She shook her head. "No. In fact, I'm wondering now if that's why he bit you."

"Huh?"

"If you were badly wounded, dying even, by biting you and infecting you, he may have saved your life."

"I really wish I could remember now," Sean said, shaking his head.

"Well, getting infected can be a pretty traumatic experience, and it looks like you went through a previous one prior to it happening. I'm not surprised you blacked out on it. With time, I'm sure it'll come back to you."

"What are you, a psychiatrist?"

Roxy laughed. "No, game design."

"Oh."

"With a minor in psychology."

"Really?"

"Well, how else are you supposed to separate the rubes from their money?" She laughed. "Let's go eat. We can talk about this later."

They went to the Carl's Jr. over by the mall because it was cheap, close, and you could walk there in fifteen minutes. The sun was already setting; Spring might be coming, but it hadn't gotten here yet, so the days were still short.

Sean ordered four double cheeseburgers.

"You that hungry?" the girl behind the counter asked.

"Oh, I'll bring the extra home to eat later," Sean said and did his best not to blush. Then Roxy ordered two with a chocolate shake.

"Track team," she told the bewildered girl, who was no doubt looking at Roxy's trim figure.

"Honestly," Sean said when they finally got their food and sat down, "I feel like I could eat it all."

Roxy nodded and started in on her own food with a will. "We burn more calories, especially when we shift."

"And here I thought it was all the sex!" Sean smirked, then laughed as Roxy blushed brightly for a change.

"That, too," she whispered, then took another bite of her burger.

They spent the next ten minutes in relative silence as they both ate. Sean really had been planning to take one of the burgers back, but his body was starving and wanted every last bit of food.

"Man, if I keep eating like this, I'm gonna go broke!" He sighed. He spied a newspaper on the next table with a picture of a rather nasty accident on the front.

"Hey, what's this?" he said, pulling the paper over.

"Hmm?" Roxy mumbled, and moved around to sit next to him as he read the article.

"Says here that a van went out of control and three people died; the driver, one who wasn't wearing his seatbelt, and another who," Sean looked up at her, "got decapitated?"

"Look at the way the doors are hanging off," she said, pointing to the picture.

"Oh my god," Sean said and felt the blood drain from his face, "you don't think that's connected to me, do you?"

"Only one way to find out," Roxy said and looked at the picture again. "You know, that's not all that far from here. East Tenth and Manhattan."

Sean looked at it, and something vaguely registered about a van, a van and blood, a lot of blood. Then it was gone.

"Are you sure?" he asked in a soft voice.

"I'm sure there'll be all sorts of folks out looking at the accident site. Humans are kinda ghoulish like that." She smirked.

"No, we're not!" he protested.

"You're not one of them anymore, Sean," Roxy said and, leaning over, she kissed him! "Remember that."

"Wow," Sean said and looked at her.

"Oh, you'll get used to it," she told him. It wasn't like he had much of a choice, after all.

"No, I mean you kissed me, in public!" Sean looked at her. "I don't think I've ever had a girlfriend do *that* before!"

"Oh well, in that case..." Roxy laughed, leaned over, and laid a nice, long, and wet one on him.

Sean got over his surprise quickly enough, until someone coughed and mumbled something about 'get a room'.

Giggling, they separated. Getting up and tossing their trash, they quickly went outside. The sun had set, but with all the lights around and the city just a mile away, it never really got that dark in Reno.

"You must have dated some pretty lousy girls," Roxy told him as they left, holding hands.

Sean shrugged. "Actually, I never really dated that much."

"Really? Why not?"

"When my father died, he left us pretty badly in debt. We lost everything we had; the house, cars, hell they even took most of my clothing and all my games! When I wasn't in school, I was working anyplace that would have me. I think I've bussed tables or washed dishes at every casino and restaurant in the city."

"How old were you?"

"I was eight when he died." Sean sighed and shook his head. "They told us it was some kind of workplace accident, but the insurance company claimed it was negligence, which effectively made it his own fault, and they refused to pay."

"Wow, that sucks!"

"Then the city came around and fined us a quarter of a million dollars because of 'unsafe conditions' at his company. The EPA fined us another couple hundred grand, and well, bills came due, and the government had already frozen all our money before seizing it.

"Don't even get me started on the IRS."

Roxy moved closer and leaned against him; she could hear in his voice that he was still pretty torn up over it.

"What did he do for a living?"

Sean shrugged. "I don't really know. My mom doesn't like to talk about it, says it's all in the past now, and we just have to continue with our lives. I think it was some kind of research, though into what, I have no idea. I just remember being at his labs once, there were all sorts of equipment and odd stuff in the building. I couldn't figure it out then, and now?" Sean shrugged. "I barely remember enough of it to even guess what anything was."

They had turned down Ninth Street by now and were walking under the bridge when a police car slowed down, the officer inside taking a look at them, then speeding back up again.

"What was that all about?" Sean wondered.

A few minutes later as they turned down Manhattan, another police car cruised by, only this one was already going slow, and the officer inside waved to them.

"Okay, that's weird, what's with all the cops?"

"Obviously there's more to the story than the one the paper had," Roxy told him, and they crossed the street, heading towards the scene of the crash.

"Wow, that's pretty obvious," Roxy said as they looked at the splintered and broken pole. Another telephone pole had been set in the ground next to it, and there was a crew working on it, moving the power lines from the old pole to the new one.

"What happened?" Sean asked one of the workers standing around with a flag, waving it at the occasional car that came down the side street.

"Some tweakers in a van hit the pole yesterday."

"A van did that?" Roxy asked in a sweet and innocent voice, almost making Sean choke.

"Yeah, they must have been going like a bat out of hell. People heard a bunch of gunshots and saw some folks running away afterward. The crew that put in the new pole said there was blood everywhere before the fire department came and washed it all down. Probably some gang-bangers fighting over drugs."

"Wow! This close to the uni?" Roxy said, still using that innocent little girl voice as she snuggled up closer to Sean, who put a protective arm around her.

"Oh, that ain't the worst of it!" the guy chuckled and winked at Sean as he waved his flag at another car.

"How does it get any worse than that?" Sean asked.

"They found an extra arm! Somewhere out there, there's a guy missing his arm!" The flagman laughed. "He's probably dead by now; they've been searching for his body all over the place."

"Umm, thanks," Sean said as Roxy started to tug him back the way they'd come.

"What's up?" he asked her as soon as they'd gotten out of earshot.

"There was a guy sitting in a car across the street that was paying way too much attention to you," Roxy whispered, steering him back toward the university.

"What?" Sean said, stunned.

Roxy sighed. "Sean, you have all these heightened senses now; you see better, hear better, and can even smell faint scents and learn things from them. You need to start using them!"

"Hey!" Sean said, feeling just a little defensive. "Yesterday I was a perfectly normal human! Give me a break; it's only been a day! I didn't grow up with this, you know!"

"I'm sorry," Roxy said, dragging him over to the bus stop; she could already see the next bus down the street a few blocks away, "but it doesn't look like you're going to be able to use that excuse for long. Something's going on, and you're in the middle of it. Besides," she said and looked him up and down with a bit of a smirk, "*now* you're perfectly normal."

Sean sighed and smiled weakly back at her. "*You* would think that, wouldn't you?"

Roxy grabbed his hands and put them on her ass as she faced him, pressing her chest against his. "Oh? And you don't?"

Sean blushed as he remembered just how the day had gone, more importantly, the entire afternoon. '*See how much better your life is with me?*' floated through the back of his head.

"Uh, yeah," Sean conceded, and leaning down, he gave Roxy a kiss that was happily returned.

"Better," she said when they finished. "Now, let's catch our bus."

"Won't this make us easier to follow?"

"Only if we're really being followed," she pointed out to him. "But the last thing we want right now is something happening with lots of witnesses around."

"But won't that stop them?" Sean asked as he followed her up the steps and into the bus. They both flashed their college ID's and bus passes, and he followed her to the very back of the bus, where it was darkest.

"They're not the ones who are being stopped," Roxy said and then gave him a grin that was all teeth and pure predator.

Sean's eyes got wide and suddenly he felt his beast sit up and start paying attention.

"Welcome to life at the *real* top of the food chain." Roxy giggled. "Now, start watching out the windows and see if anyone's following this bus."

They had just turned on to York when Sean spotted the car. A large black Ford Flex, and it was definitely following the bus.

"I see them," he told Roxy.

"Hard to follow a bus through a neighborhood and not be seen, isn't it?"

"You sound like you've done this before," Sean grumbled.

"Hunting and tracking are two of the biggest games I used to play as a child." She shrugged. "We have all the advantages, it's just learning how to best use them, while keeping everything out of sight of the norms. Right now, they think they're hunting us," she smiled showing her teeth again in a shockingly feral grin, "and we're going to let them keep thinking that, right up until the moment it isn't to our advantage anymore."

Sean suddenly realized that Roxy was probably thinking about killing the people in that car following them. This wasn't a game of hide and seek, or even tag. This wasn't going to end with words, or a fistfight and maybe some bruises. This was for real, this was life or death, and she seemed more excited than worried.

'This is what I was meant for'. His beast had obviously found his voice, and he could feel him stretching inside him, getting ready for the fight, the hunt, the kill.

"Is this right?" he asked Roxy, concerned at the thought of what was going to happen.

'Of course it's right!' his beast growled deep in his chest.

"Of course it's right," Roxy echoed. "They mean us harm; they've probably harmed you already. What's your beast telling you?"

"Huh?"

"Your lion, what's he telling you?"

'To fight them, kill them, we must protect ourselves and our pride!'

"The same thing you are," Sean admitted. "He wants to take them out."

Roxy nodded, and reaching out with a finger, she tapped him on the nose, "Listen to him. There are times to restrain your beast, your lion; this isn't going to be one of them. If it gets to be too much for you, set him free. Just don't hide from what's going on; he'll need your guidance, your intelligence. You're a team, you need to work together."

'Our mate is wise, listen to her.'

Sean blushed at that.

Roxy smirked. "What did he say?"

"To listen to you," Sean replied, still blushing.

"Oh? Is that all?" she teased him.

"Um, I think he has designs on you," he admitted.

Surprisingly, to him at least, Roxy laughed. "Yeah, he's a lion. They do that."

"It's just weird, having this second voice in my head."

"Don't worry, as you spend more time together, you'll integrate back into one person. Right now you're still finding your way."

"Getting back to the guys in the car, what do we do now?"

"We get off at the school, then run to the high school behind it. It's dark out now, so no one will be there, and it'll give us the space to deal with them."

"What about the," Sean looked around, there was no one sitting back by them fortunately, but still he lowered his voice, "the bodies."

"Don't claw anyone up, don't bite anyone. As long as it doesn't look like an animal killed them, it'll just get chalked up to gang violence or a drug deal gone bad."

Sean nodded and thought about that. He knew from his run-in with Dean this morning that he was now stronger and faster than them.

"What if they have guns?" he asked the moment the idea popped into his head.

"It hurts, but you'll get over it," Roxy said, watching the stops as they turned onto G Street.

"What if they have silver bullets?"

"Then don't let them hit you," she said, and hitting the stop buzzer, she got up.

"Come on, this is it."

Saturday Night's Alright for Fighting

The second the door to the bus opened; Roxy jumped out and took off, laughing.

"Come on, slowpoke!" she yelled, making it look for all the world like they were playing a game as she quickly scaled and vaulted over the chain link fence.

Sean chased after her, not really sure what the plan was, but he sure as hell knew enough *not* to look at the car that had been following the bus.

They ran under the trees and through the playground, stopping briefly to kiss, then running on again. He heard the car pull into the school parking lot as the bus pulled away from the curb. Of course, the car had rammed the closed chain link gate, breaking it open, so it hadn't been exactly quiet. Roxy ignored it, so he did, too, as they ran across the field.

The gate at the other end was open, so they both ran through it, then Roxy stopped and turned towards him.

"Grab me and make it look like we're making out," she whispered.

Sean was more than willing to do so.

"Okay, they're catching up. Take my hand, and let's go!"

Sean grabbed her hand, and they both ran across the street and through the open gate into the school parking lot; there were a few cars here. He figured it was probably the janitors or something; it was after seven now, and full dark had descended. Well, as dark as it got in Reno. But he was surprised he was having no trouble seeing at all.

As they continued to run, he heard the car pull in behind them; they were passing the buildings on their left and covered parking on the right. He could hear the car following them, it was getting closer, but they weren't rushing. Sean guessed they liked the idea of going someplace more private, too.

Soon they were running on dirt, and Roxy dragged him behind a building.

"Get ready," she growled, and when Sean looked at her, he saw that Roxy had shifted into her hybrid form. Her feet were bare, the loose pants were now skin-tight, and her t-shirt looked like it was about to split.

If there hadn't been a bunch of men chasing them, Sean would have had other things on his mind.

"Later, if you're a good boy," Roxy growled.

Sean blushed and turned back, waiting at the corner of the building. They heard the car stop and the doors open, then footsteps.

'Four,' his beast identified, and Sean knew he was right.

When the first one stepped into view, Sean looked him over. He was wearing slacks, a nice shirt, and a light suit jacket. The reason for the jacket was clear; he had a Glock in his right hand.

'Wait.'

"Come on out kids, we only want to talk to Sean," the man said in a slightly accented voice.

A second one came into sight as he and Roxy crouched in the shadows behind the building. He was dressed in a similar fashion, and also had a pistol, another Glock.

"Sean," the first one said again, pulling out a flashlight, "don't make this any harder than it has…"

'Attack!'

Sean jumped out and grabbed the one talking by the throat as a third one was stepping into sight. A gun went off instantly, and he felt a burning sensation in his leg.

"Don't shoot him, you asshole!" one of the others yelled, and Sean stumbled a moment trying to grab the gun hand of the guy he had by the throat as several other shots went off. He could see that Roxy was making rather quick work of one of them, as she broke his arm, pushed his pistol up under his chin, and pulled the trigger.

But the others were shooting at *her*!

'Let go!' his beast roared at him as he saw Roxy get shot.

He let go.

It was almost surreal. One moment he had his hand grabbing a man's throat as he tried to strangle him, and the next he was on his hind legs as he pulled a paw the size of a dinner plate back from the man's head.

'No claws!' he warned his lion, who instead of ripping the man's face off, smacked him in the side of the head instead.

Sean heard the man's neck snapping as his lion dropped down to all fours and charged one of the men shooting at Roxy. He could hear his beast's thoughts, which were clear and simple: *kill*.

As he attacked the shooter, it dawned on Sean that his lion was pretty freaking big. He slammed this man in the side with a paw and sent him flying into a wall, which he hit hard, and slid down to the ground, in a daze. Spinning to face the other one, he was surprised to see that Roxy was now pointing one of the Glocks at him, point-blank. The expression on his face as he looked at her, and then at him, made it very clear that this was not what they'd been expecting.

"Who sent you?" Roxy growled.

"I can't…"

Roxy shot the guy Sean's lion had slammed against the wall twice, stopping him from moving ever again. She then put the gun in the guy's face again before he had a chance to even raise his and aim it at her.

"Talk."

"Sawyer," the man gulped.

"See? That wasn't hard, was it?" Roxy said, then shot him in the chest.

Sean was shocked. He couldn't believe she'd do such a thing! The man looked up at her, shocked as well, as he slowly collapsed.

"I know Sawyer," Roxy said, "you don't work for him."

With that she gave him the coup de grace and shot him in the head.

"Get their guns," she said, then looking over at him, she stopped and giggled. "You look funny like that!"

"What?" his beast growled, and Sean yelled at him *not* to growl at Roxy.

"Your clothes are still on," she giggled, "or what's left of them, at least!

"Let's move, I hear sirens."

She was right, Sean could hear them too. He grabbed the pistol out of one of the guy's hands while Roxy gathered up the other three, as well as taking their wallets.

"Come on!" she said and took off running to the north, across the baseball field. Keeping up with her wasn't easy; cheetahs were fast, and lions weren't.

When they started to jump over fences – at least he could do that easily – he caught up with her.

She led him past the library then, waiting for a break in traffic, they dodged across Twelfth. Sticking to the trees, they stayed out of sight of the main road and followed it along until they came to a bunch of older apartment buildings, where they hunkered down for a bit.

Gathering up the pistols, Roxy looked at him. She was back in her human form, there were some flecks of blood on her shirt, but that seemed to be all.

"I'd try to get you to shift back, but you'd be all but naked then. At least as a lion, your coloration blends in with the ground."

Sean watched through his lion's eyes, as he looked himself over and saw the shreds of clothing still wrapped around his body.

"Well, let me get all that off of you," Roxy said, and he felt his big head nod as he stood there, enjoying the feeling of his woman's hands as she stripped off his clothing.

'*My woman?*' Sean thought.

'*You don't like her?*' came his lion's response.

'*Don't be silly.*'

'I wasn't, you were.'

'We need to talk about our attitudes towards women.' Sean sighed mentally.

'Yes, you have much to learn!' His lion chuffed a little.

"Hmm?" Roxy asked. She was going through his pockets and getting his wallet, keys, and phone.

"Talking to my human."

Roxy snickered. "Oh, one of *those* moments!"

"You have had these problems too?"

"Sooner or later, we've all had them. The first step is for the two of you to realize that you're really the same person. After you stop second-guessing each other, it gets easier."

Sean felt his head nod again, and he settled down.

'Now what?' he asked.

"Now what?" his lion echoed.

"Now we play duck and dodge and find a good place to hole up until the traffic lightens up. Then we sneak back home and go to bed."

Roxy held up his ruined sneakers then, "Weren't these new?"

Sean sighed and facepalmed, causing Roxy to giggle again, and surprising himself and his lion with their cooperation.

It was after midnight when they finally made it back to the house they had their rooms in.

"I'll go in first," Roxy told him. "Once things are clear, I'll wave out the window of your room. Okay?"

They nodded, or perhaps, he nodded? Spending the night running around as a lion had been educational. He'd gained an appreciation for his lion body, and the mind that inhabited it. There were many times when the lion wasn't sure what to do and he'd just filled it in, instantly. He found he still had a certain amount of control, not over the body so much yet, but over the decisions of what to do with it.

He recalled his fight with Dean then, how he'd been able to just 'do' what needed to be done. The lion had been guiding him then, just as he was guiding the lion now. He'd given in to it then, because he hadn't realized what was happening.

'And it worked,' his lion told him.

Sean had to agree, it had worked. Arguing with success was stupid; thankfully, Roxy was more than willing to help educate him, at least. Once he'd gotten used to letting his lion run, as she called it, he'd found it quite enjoyable.

Then, of course, there were his lion senses. At first, a lot of it hadn't made any sense, but his lion side interpreted it all for him, and as the night wore on, he understood. He could feel everything his lion felt, the wind, the ground, the feeling of his strong muscles and heavy body. Hear what he heard, smell what he smelled, and boy did he smell a lot! Sean had had no idea the world was so full of different and interesting scents. Sure, it was a little weird; he almost felt like a backseat driver at times, but not quite.

Roxy took her sneakers back off and shifted again into her hybrid form before she opened the door. She wanted her senses to be at their best. These people knew who Sean was, so they had to know where he lived. But they hadn't been around here for some reason, preferring to go after him when he was away from the house.

Opening the door, she could tell that no one had been in the hallways recently. Then again, from the sounds of it, more than a few of the residents had hooked up for the night.

Making her way upstairs quickly, she took a few minutes to check out her own room first. Everything there was in order. Listening at the wall between her room and Sean's, silence was all she heard.

Going back out into the hallway and listening at his door, it was still quiet, and she didn't smell any strange scents. Opening it, she walked inside, and after a quick examination she found everything was as they'd left it.

Waving out the window, it only took a moment before Sean pulled himself through in his full lion form. She smiled down at him; he had to weigh at least four hundred pounds, probably closer to five. His mane was as black as the hair on his head in human form, and honestly, he was a damn handsome cat. Cheetahs tended to be sleek and slender, two words that did *not* describe Sean.

"What are you staring at?" he asked in the low, rumbling, and very thick voice his lion had.

"One hella sexy cat," she said, grinning, then laughed as he started to purr.

"So, gonna' shift back?"

He shook his head; the effect on his mane was rather interesting.

"Well, we'd better clean up those bloody rags on the floor from yesterday," Roxy sighed, "before anybody gets any ideas. Then it's off to bed."

"Hmmm, bed." He purred.

"You're not planning on sleeping in my bed with me tonight like *that*, are you?" Roxy asked.

Sean just stood there and purred, smiling at her.

"And what does your 'human' have to say about that?" Roxy teased.

"Hmmm, bed."

Roxy rolled her eyes and sighed. She was pleased to see they were agreeing with each other, at least. She just hoped her bed could handle the weight.

Sunday Morning won't be the Same

Sean woke up a little groggily; mornings were apparently still not his best time of the day. Opening his eyes, he looked up at the ceiling and started, just as he realized there was someone cuddled up against him, this was *not* his room, and *not* his bed.

Looking over at Roxy's naked body as she pressed up against him in her sleep, he remembered where he was and what had happened to him yesterday. He'd shifted back at some point during the night, when Roxy had started to get frisky, but she'd made it rather clear that he had to shift back first before things went any farther.

He'd found it to be rather simple. He had simply *done* it. His lion didn't fight him, he was feeling a little frisky too, and what he felt, the lion felt. Because while they were different, they were still the same person.

Yeah, Sean realized he'd have to think about that more. Roxy said it would come with time and experience.

He heard it then, someone was knocking on a door.

"Sean Valens, this is detective Schumer! Please open the door."

"Oh shit," Roxy grumbled, rolling out of bed.

"Yeah," Sean agreed, standing up, "I don't have any clothes in here!"

"You left your robe in here yesterday," Roxy said, moving over to the back of the door where it was hanging. Grabbing it, she tossed it to him, and he quickly put it on while she donned her own.

"Mr. Valens!" he heard again, followed by more knocking.

Opening the door, Sean leaned out and looked at the man knocking on his door. Actually, there were two of them. One was dressed in a plain suit with a badge hanging out of the breast pocket; the other was wearing a uniform. Sean noticed that George, the other guy living on the floor, was looking out of his door, and when George saw him stick my head out of Roxy's room, his eyes got wide.

"What do you want?" Sean grumbled. "It's early."

They both turned towards him. "Are you Sean Valens?" the one in the suit, obviously the detective, asked him.

Sean nodded. "Yeah, that's me."

"Do you have any ID? We were told that this was your room," he said and nodded toward his door.

"It is; this is my girlfriend's room." Stretching, Sean walked out of Roxy's room and, going over to his, he opened the unlocked door and went inside.

"We've been trying to call you since last night," Detective Schumer said.

"Yeah, I think my phone's dead," Sean said. Picking it up and opening it, he noticed the battery was completely discharged. "I forgot to charge it."

"How do you forget to charge your phone?" the uniformed officer asked.

Sean turned and smiled at him. "New girlfriend." He nodded at Roxy, who was standing in the door wearing only her bathrobe and looking very good in it as she blushed.

"Oh," was all the officer could say, but Sean noticed he was smiling.

"So, what's this all about then," Sean asked and, yawning, sat on his bed.

"Do you know a Gregory Sampson?" Detective Schumer asked him.

"Yeah, I've known Sampson," Sean thought about it, "I think all my life. He lives next door to my mom, works at the same casino. Why?"

"He's dead."

Sean didn't even remember jumping to his feet as he stared at the detective, "What! What do you mean dead? What happened? What?" Sean had to restrain himself from grabbing the detective, who was looking at him, concerned.

"Were you two close?"

"After my father died, he helped us out with a lot of things. He used to work for my dad; they were like best friends or something. He was like a big brother to me, always there when I needed help." Sean sighed and shook his head; something in the back of his mind was bothering him about this, but he didn't know what.

"I can't believe he's dead! I talked to him last weekend. What happened?"

"We found his body yesterday morning, a couple miles from here."

"What do you mean, you found his body?"

"He'd been shot five times. Near as we can figure it, he came across something he shouldn't have. There were no drugs on him or in his system."

Sean snorted. "Sampson didn't even drink, no way he'd ever have anything to do with drugs." Shaking his head, he sat back down on his bed. "Mom is going to be devastated," he looked up at the detective, "have you told her yet? If not, can you give me a ride over there?"

"Well see, that's part of the problem," Detective Schumer started off.

Sean was back on his feet, and this time, he'd grabbed the detective's arms and was staring him right in the face.

"What. Do. You. Mean?" he said slowly.

"We haven't been able to find your mother since yesterday."

"What!?"

"She's not at work, not at home; there are no signs of forced entry. We haven't gone inside yet, we're still waiting on a search warrant and it hasn't been long enough to declare her a missing person yet."

The Detective looked at Sean. "So, I was hoping…?"

"Let me get dressed," Sean said, looking around for some clean clothes.

"Um, maybe you might want to shower first?" the uniformed officer suggested.

Sean stopped and looked down at himself. Yeah, he needed a shower.

"Wait here, don't touch anything, I'll be right back!" Grabbing a towel, he headed for the shower. He hadn't even realized Roxy had followed him until she pushed him to the back of the shower and got inside with him.

"What are you doing?" he hissed softly.

"Going with you, what do you think?" she hissed back.

Sean sighed and kissed her. "Thank you."

Ten minutes later they were dressed and sitting in the back of the police car as they drove over to his mother's house. The detective had balked at first when Sean grabbed his girlfriend, but Sean just told him it wasn't up for discussion and changed the subject by asking why they'd searched his room while he was in the shower.

The detective looked embarrassed, and the uniformed officer just smirked. That was the end of the discussion.

The drive to Sean's mother's place wasn't all that long, especially this early on a Sunday morning. Sean just sat there, holding Roxy's hand and wondering what the hell was going on. If only he'd called her, warned her.

But warned her of what? It wasn't until last night that he'd known anyone was after him, and Sampson lived next door, he'd have run off anyone who'd have even thought of giving her any trouble.

Sean shook his head; none of this made any sense. He was just a poor kid going to school to try and get a decent paying job after spending his life in poverty. Suddenly, everything was happening to him, and he had no idea why. There had to be an answer to all of this, somewhere. But where?

He suspected his missing memory from Friday had something to do with it. Because up until that moment, his life had been plain. Boring, in fact.

They pulled into the trailer park that had been Sean's home from the time he was nine until he'd moved out two years ago. He looked over at Roxy and could see the look of surprise on her face. He'd told her he was poor, but seeing was believing. At least the people here took care of their places, so it wasn't a run-down mess.

They pulled up in front of his mom's place. There was a patrol car sitting out front; he was sure the neighbors would just be loving that. Getting out of the back of the car, the first thing he noticed was his mother's car was gone.

"Her car's gone," he said, looking at the detective.

"We found it parked at the casino, in the employees' parking lot," he said. "Both of the front tires were flat."

"Flat?"

"Yeah, both were slashed."

Shaking his head, Sean walked up to the door, got his keys out, and put them in the lock.

"Wait out here," he said to the detective.

"What?" the detective said, looking surprised.

"If my Mom is just laying in bed sick, the last thing I want to do is drag a bunch of cops inside," Sean said, staring at the man.

"Okay," he grumbled but didn't push it.

"Roxy, come on," Sean said. Pushing the door open, he stepped inside.

The place had been trashed, there was stuff thrown around everywhere. Someone had obviously been looking for something. What, Sean had no idea.

"I take it this isn't normal?" Roxy asked, and Sean glared at her.

"Hey, your room isn't all that much better," she said, giving him a weak smile.

"Mom is a neat freak. Let's check her bedroom."

The place wasn't all that big; it was only a single-wide trailer, after all. There were only two bedrooms; his was on the left as they walked towards the back. The door was open, and the room was just as tossed as the rest of the house. Same for the bathroom after that.

The door to the master bedroom was open, and again, everything in it had been tossed over pretty well.

"Smell anything?" Sean asked, looking around.

"Those cops still outside?" Roxy asked.

Sean nodded.

"Give me a moment," she said. Walking into the bedroom, he watched as she kicked her shoes off and shifted to her hybrid form.

"Better nose," she said and winked, then dropped to her knees and started sniffing around the room.

"You okay in there?" he heard the detective call from outside.

"Yeah, just a minute," Sean said and looked around the room. Nothing was really broken; someone had obviously been searching for something.

"Okay," Roxy said, putting her shoes back on, and came over to him.

"Well, let's go let the cops in." Sean sighed and headed back to the front door.

"Come on in; she's not here, but somebody else has been."

"Looks like somebody was looking for something," Detective Schumer said, looking around the room.

"There's nothing here to be found," Sean said, "my mom spent ten years paying off the tax liens the IRS hit us with after my father died. It's only been in the last two years that she's even started to have any extra money at all."

"Why didn't you declare bankruptcy?" Roxy asked.

"We did. IRS debts don't go away, even in a bankruptcy."

"Yeah," Detective Schumer said, looking around, "they're real bastards that way. Do you mind if I have a look around?"

Sean sighed and shook his head. "Knock yourself out, Detective. Have you been inside Sampson's house yet?"

"Actually, no. Do you have a key?"

"Don't need one, he never locks his door."

Detective Schumer looked at him in surprise. "He never locked his door? Here?"

Sean shrugged. "We may be poor, but the people around here don't steal and, well, you don't mess with Sampson. He always knew who was doing what, and he didn't care much for thieves."

Walking out the front door and going across the narrow driveway, Sean walked up the steps to Sampson's place and opened the door. It had obviously been searched as well, though Sampson had a lot less stuff in his home, another single-wide trailer like Sean's mom's.

Walking towards the back, he opened the door to the master bedroom, which was closed.

There were two dead bodies in the room.

"Son of a bitch," Detective Schumer said. "Who are those guys?"

"I guess Sampson caught them in the act," Sean said, looking them over. Both appeared to be dressed about the same as the four they'd run into last night. He noticed a Glock lying on the floor by one of them, and while a lot of people used Glocks, this group all seemed to favor them.

"This just became a crime scene," Detective Schumer told him. "I'm going to have to ask you to step outside."

Sean just sighed and, taking Roxy's hand, they went back out to sit on the hood of the unmarked car they'd come in. Over the next hour, they watched as several more police cars showed up, Along with a van from the morgue and another van from what looked like the forensics team.

Eventually Detective Schumer came back over to them.

"I'm sorry you had to see that, but I guess you're right about them having been caught in the act. Was Sampson some kind of martial artist or something?"

"Why?" Sean asked.

"One of the victims had his throat crushed; the other had a broken neck."

Sean nodded. "I think he was a commando or something. But yeah, he was a pretty tough guy and knew how to fight. Like I said earlier, you don't mess with Sampson." Sean sighed heavily then and put his head in his hands. "Or at least, you *didn't*."

"Sorry, Kid," Detective Schumer said. "I really hate to be the bearer of bad news but, well, at least he got two of them. Do you have any idea what this may have been about?"

"No."

"Did your mother or Mr. Sampson have any enemies?"

Sean shook his head. "My mom was too poor to have any, and well, Sampson may have, but I never heard about it."

"Do you think you could come down to the morgue and ID his body for us at least?"

Sean sighed and nodded. "Sure," he said. Getting up, he and Roxy got back in the car again.

The ride over to the city morgue was a somber one. Sean wasn't sure which was bothering him more, that his mother was missing, or that Sampson was dead. There was always a chance his mother would turn up alive and okay. But Sampson was dead, and that was final. Roxy had pulled his head down against her shoulder and was holding him. It felt nice to have someone to hold you at a time like this.

When they got to the morgue, Detective Schumer asked her if she wanted to wait outside while they identified the body.

"No, I'll go with him," Roxy said, tightening her grip on Sean's hand.

"It isn't pretty," the detective warned her.

"It never is." Roxy sighed.

The detective looked at her, a little surprised.

"You have experience with dead bodies?" he asked, looking at her a little suspiciously.

"My mom's a medical examiner in Vegas," Roxy said, surprising the Detective, as well as Sean, who'd had no idea.

"And," she added, "my dad's the sheriff."

"One of the deputies?" Detective Schumer asked.

"No, *the Sheriff*. Sheriff Channing is my father."

"Oh, well, ah…"

Sean looked at her. "If you're from Vegas, why didn't you go to UNLV?"

"Because dad checking out all of my boyfriends in high school was bad enough. No way was I going to put up with it in college."

Sean nodded, and they followed Detective Schumer into the back of the building, to a room filled with those square metal doors that, up till now, he'd only ever seen in the movies.

Grabbing the handle on one of them, Detective Schumer unlatched the door and pulled it out. Just like in the movies, it came open like a filing cabinet. Only this one had a man lying in it, and he was cold.

Grabbing the sheet covering the body, Sean flipped it back to expose the face. It was Sampson. He spent a moment just staring at the man, who'd at times been his best friend, and others almost like a father to him.

"I'm sorry I never got to meet him." Roxy sighed, standing next to Sean and looking at Sampson's body. Reaching up, she touched his face a moment, then withdrew her hand.

"Does he have any family?" Detective Schumer asked. "We weren't able to find anyone other than your mother and you."

Sean shook his head. "No, as I understand it, he came here from Rhodesia after the government fell. I don't think he had any family left, after that."

Closing the drawer, the Detective led them back out of the building.

"I'll call you if we learn anything. Here's my card; please call me if you can think of anything that might help, or if you hear from your mother."

"Thanks, I will."

"Do you two need a ride back?"

Sean shook his head. "No, we can walk from here, and I could use some fresh air."

"Okay, take care of yourself, Son."

"Thanks," Sean said, putting the detective's card in his pocket.

Walking out of the building, Sean just looked around a moment, feeling lost.

"Come on," Roxy said, grabbing him and dragging him in the opposite direction of their respective rooms. "You look like death, and we haven't had a thing to eat since last night."

Sean nodded and sighed. "Why would anyone kidnap my mom?"

"I don't know, but I do know one thing."

"What? You picked up someone's scent at my mom's?"

"Not that; it was the same guys we found dead in Sampson's house. Obviously they didn't find what they were after in your place, and went there next. No, this is something a little more important than that."

"What?"

"Sampson is the one who turned you."

"What?!" Sean stopped and looked at her.

"He was a werelion. I wasn't sure; I could smell it in his house, but I wanted to be *sure*.

That's why I touched him, to get his scent. They keep it so cold down there that smells don't travel far."

"You can tell from his scent that he's the one who bit me?"

Roxy nodded. "Yup. Also, the blood on your clothes? Some of it was his. Whatever happened to you Friday night, Sampson was involved in it."

"Sampson would never hurt me!" Sean fumed, defending his dead friend.

"Who said he hurt you?" Roxy said, grabbing his hand and leading him off again. Lycans got testy when they were hungry. She figured getting some food into him would help calm him down. Plus, she was starting to feel a little edgy herself.

"It could be that he got shot saving you. Whoever shot him was using silver bullets; that's one of the sure ways of stopping a lycan."

"Maybe it was those guys with the Glocks?"

"No, silver bullets have to be hand-loaded, and well, Glocks don't do well with reloaded bullets. They have a tendency to fail rather spectacularly."

"So, he pulled me from that van then?"

"Probably, but first things first," she said and dragged him inside the Denny's. "Let's eat."

Questions and More Questions

Sean picked at his food at first; he hadn't ordered all that much, while Roxy had ordered probably four times as much as he had.

"So, what do we know?" Roxy asked him.

"Well, we know something happened to me Friday; we think I was kidnapped in that van that crashed."

"With the way someone was watching that site to see if you came back to investigate it, I think it's a safe bet you were in it," Roxy said.

"Okay, and we believe a lycan, or something similar, caused it to crash and ripped the doors off, saving me."

"Which we now know to be Sampson," Roxy pointed out and looked pointedly at his food, then at him.

Sean smiled wanly and started to eat.

"We also know that they searched your house, Sampson's house, but oddly enough, not your apartment. Hell, they haven't even come *by* your apartment."

"And we know they don't work for Sawyer," Sean said between bites. "By the way, who the hell is Sawyer?"

"Someone you're not ready to meet yet."

"How'd you know they didn't work for him?"

"Because Sawyer doesn't hire humans." Roxy shrugged. "My dad ran him out of Vegas years ago. He's a goblin; he buys and sells a lot of arcane stuff, he's a fence for the supernatural. Pretty involved in the rackets and some other shady things, too, I'm sure. But he hates humans with a passion."

Sean looked up at Roxy. "Wait, there are *goblins* out there?"

Roxy chuckled. "Of course there are! What, did you think lycans were all that existed?"

"Well, how come I've never heard of it?"

"Same reason you never heard about lycans and were-creatures before, of course," Roxy told him. "Humans aren't very accepting of other races or things they don't understand."

Sean nodded. "I've noticed."

"So not a lot of people know about us, and we all kinda keep a low profile."

"Well, how does he feel about lycans?" Looking down, Sean saw his plate was now empty. He also realized he was still hungry.

Roxy shrugged. "Depends." Picking up the plate of sausages she'd ordered, she dumped it on his plate.

"What? That's your food!" Sean protested.

"No," she said and followed it with the plate of extra bacon she'd ordered, "it's your food. I knew your mind wasn't on eating, so I ordered extra. Eat."

"But, I," Sean looked at the food and tried not to drool all over it, "I can't, you paid for it! I can pay my own way!"

"Sean?" Roxy said smiling sweetly.

"I'm serious, Roxy."

"It's the females of the pride's duty to make sure that their male is fed. Ask your lion. Now, eat."

"Wait, are you saying you're…"

'*Told you! Now eat!*'

"Sure looks that way." Roxy winked as Sean started in on the food with a will.

"But you're not a lioness," he said between bites.

'Doesn't matter.'

"Doesn't matter," she said, echoing his lion. "As long as we're the same genus, it works out. It's actually not all that uncommon."

"Huh," was all Sean could say as he looked at Roxy, watching her as he ate, until suddenly she blushed.

"What?" she asked, looking at him.

"I think I'm going to like being a lion." He smirked.

"Yeah, me too!" Roxy giggled and winked.

"So, do you think this Sawyer might know why everyone's after me?" Sean asked as he finished off the sausages and the bacon. He was eyeing the extra plate of pancakes, so she shoved it over in front of him as she finished the food on her own plate.

"I don't know. He might. But I'm a bit hesitant to ask."

"Why?" Sean asked around a forkful of pancakes.

"Because if it's something really expensive, or important, or worth a lot of money, he just might decide to take it for himself."

"Oh?"

Roxy nodded. "Goblins are greedy that way."

"But if it's something that only humans want, he may tell us just to screw them over," Sean pointed out.

"Yeah, he might. But I'd rather leave him as a last resort."

"Are there any other options out there?"

"Wellll, there's one. But I'm not sure about it yet."

"Why not?"

"I have a friend who's a witch. But I'm not sure I want you to meet her just yet."

Sean set down his fork. "There are witches, too?"

Roxy laughed and nodded. "And wizards, and warlocks, and magic users of all stripes. But they're almost all human. They even have a little council, well, the good ones do, at least."

"And you have a friend who's a witch?"

Roxy nodded, smiling. "Yup."

Picking his fork up, Sean went back to work finishing off the pancakes.

"So why don't you want me to meet her?"

"Because you're still new. I'd like you to be a little more comfortable with your new self and your lion before exposing you to her." Roxy shrugged. "She's a bit intense."

Sean nodded and finished off the pancakes, then drained his glass of water.

"So," he said, summing it up, "we know that someone's after me, but not who or why. We know Sampson infected me, but not why. We know my mom is missing, and it's probably related."

"We already agreed that we think he bit you to save your life," Roxy pointed out.

Sean nodded. "It makes sense, especially if he was dying from being shot."

"Maybe they're after something your father left you?"

Sean shook his head. "No, they took everything we had. The house, cars, furniture, all my mom's jewelry. Like I said, they even took half my clothing and all my toys. They left us completely destitute. Anything my dad gave me was taken away twelve years ago."

"Well, they searched Sampson's house too. Maybe it was something *he* had?"

"Then why come after me?"

Roxy just shook her head. "I have no idea."

"Well, let's go back home. My phone is probably full of messages by now. I was supposed to go gaming with my friends last night."

"Oh? Why didn't you?" Roxy smirked.

"It was a matter of my pride," Sean said with a wink, causing Roxy to laugh.

They were sitting in his room, or rather Roxy was sitting at his desk while he cleaned things up. It wasn't that his room was actually dirty, he just had a tendency to stack things on the floor rather than putting them away. With his clothes in the washing machine downstairs, it helped; he realized he was going to have to start keeping his room a bit cleaner now that he had a girlfriend.

"I'm down to three pairs of pants now," Sean sighed as he put his books back on the shelf and sat down on his bed, "and I need to go buy *another* pair of sneakers!"

"A slight wardrobe change might be required," Roxy said, grinning.

"I'm not wearing spandex!" Sean grumbled and picked up his phone to check his messages.

"I was thinking something more like a canvas loafer or deck shoes," Roxy said, "or even moccasins, then at least they'll come off your feet and you won't ruin them."

Sean pondered that and nodded. "That would work. Still, my socks will be trashed, and what about my pants and shirts?"

"Well, loose button-down shirts will still fit after you shift. You may pop a few buttons, but that's easy to fix. As for pants," she shrugged, "start wearing cargo pants and don't use a belt. Then there's a chance they'll fall off as you shift."

"Still, it isn't going to be cheap, and I don't have a lot of money." Sean shook his head. "I wish I'd thought to grab some clothes while we were at my mom's."

"I don't think that would've looked good to the police," Roxy pointed out, "besides, you're not broke; you've got almost six hundred dollars in cash!"

Sean looked at her. "What are you talking about?"

"I emptied the wallets of those four guys who attacked us last night." She shrugged. "Not like they needed it anymore."

"But that's *stealing*!"

'*Quit being stupid,*' his lion spoke up.

"Quit being stupid," Roxy laughed, "to the victor go the spoils, and we didn't start that fight. They did."

"I hate when you do that," Sean grumbled some more.

"Do what?"

"Say the exact same thing my lion does."

Roxy giggled then, and rather adorably, too. "No wonder my beast likes yours so much. We're on the same wavelength."

Sean sighed and rolled his eyes. "And another thing, did you really have to shoot that guy in cold blood like that?" he asked in a lowered voice.

Roxy nodded. "Never give a killer a second chance to kill you. Besides, your only advantage right now is that no one knows you're a lycan. The moment they figure that out, the silver bullets are going to come out."

'She's right you know.'

"Yeah, I know." Sean sighed, responding to both of them. "I just don't like it."

"I don't like it much either, Sean. But when you're fighting for survival, 'like' and 'don't like' goes right out the window. My beast pulled that trigger; yeah, I let her do it. I let her do all of the nasty things I might not want to do."

"Well, if I can get mine to take care of the laundry, it just might be worth it," Sean joked.

'Not a chance!'

"Good luck with that!" Roxy laughed.

Sean looked back at his phone; there were messages from both Chad and Alex, wondering where he was.

Holding his phone up, he turned on the camera and pointed it at Roxy.

"Say cheese," he told her, and Roxy immediately struck a sexy pose.

"Bragging?" she asked after he took the picture and sent a reply to his friends.

"They wanted to know where I was last night," Sean said, looking up and smiling at her. "I think that picture will stop any questions."

"Ha!" Roxy laughed. "More likely you'll get deluged with them now!"

As soon as she said it, his phone started to vibrate. Looking back at it, messages were coming fast and furious from both Chad and Alex, wanting to know where he'd met a gal like *that!* Was he sleeping with her? What was her name? When could they meet her?

John pinged him wanting to know if she had a sister, while Zack, Steve, *and* Teri all congratulated him on finally hooking up with someone.

"Damn, I didn't even text them!" he mumbled to himself.

"News travels fast, doesn't it?" She giggled.

"Apparently."

"Yeah, I'm just waiting for the inevitable phone call from my father."

"Why, did you tell your friends about me?" Sean asked.

"Nope, not yet. But I know that detective is going to call my dad at some point to let him know that my boyfriend is involved in a *criminal investigation.*"

"You think he will?"

Roxy laughed; Sean had to admit, he liked the sound of it, and that she was always so cheerful and happy.

"My dad is the biggest and most powerful sheriff in the state. It's Las Vegas! Of course he'll call him."

Sean thought about that a moment as something else occurred to him. "Is he a werecheetah like you?"

Roxy nodded. "Of course!"

"So you were born this way, you weren't bit like me?"

"Nope. It's pretty rare for a lycan to bite someone and infect them. My whole family are lycans, like me."

"Umm, does that mean if I bite someone, they'll get infected, too?"

Roxy shook her head. "No, you have to intentionally infect them. I wouldn't worry about it all that much just yet. Until you can shift into your hybrid form, you won't be able to infect anyone."

"That's a relief." Sean sighed and texted his friends back, telling them that her name was Roxy, and he'd bring her around next weekend.

"Oh, do you like anime?" he asked her.

"Sure, why?"

"'Cause I just told them all I'd bring you by next Friday." Sean sighed, then looked a little embarrassed. "Wow, I take you on a date to hang out with a bunch of geeks and nerds and show you off. No wonder I haven't had many girlfriends!"

Roxy snickered and burst out laughing. "I think we've sort of passed the 'initial dating stage', don't you?"

"Yeah, but it doesn't mean I don't want to take you out and actually *do* that," Sean replied, blushing. "Just because we're sleeping together, and my lion is telling me you're mine now, it doesn't mean I don't want to go out and date."

"He said that, did he?" Roxy teased, looking back at him a little coyly.

"Umm, ahh…" Sean gulped as he realized what he'd just said.

"Well, you can tell him, just because you have me on the hook, it doesn't mean you've reeled me in yet."

'*Liar.*'

"Umm." Sean blushed again. "Let's just say he feels rather strongly about you."

"And what about you?" Roxy asked demurely.

Reaching over, Sean grabbed her hand and pulled her to him and, falling back onto the bed, he kissed her.

"Let's just say that I feel a lot stronger about it than he does." He chuckled and started to slip his hands up under her shirt as he kissed her.

"Oh, I like that...oh, shit," Roxy swore as the timer they'd set for the laundry went off.

Grumbling, Sean let her get up, and got up as well.

"At least the dryer takes longer!" Roxy giggled, then spotted the watch by his clock.

"Wow, a mechanical watch? Don't see them much these days."

"Yeah, Sampson gave it to me for my birthday a few years ago."

"Why don't you wear it?"

"The band's broken, and it uses one of those fancy expanding 'twist flex' bracelets. Haven't had the money to replace it."

"Did it used to be his?" Roxy asked.

"Yeah, actually. Why?"

"'Cause that's the kind of thing shifters wear. Expanding bracelets that is. Otherwise you're always losing your watch."

"Huh. You know, he always used to wear cargo pants with stretch waistbands, too."

Roxy grinned. "Told you! What do you say, after we finish with the laundry, we go do some shopping?"

Sean nodded. "Sure."

"And bring the watch, we can find a new bracelet for it."

Fathers and Daughters

Roxy was waiting for Sean as he tried on the new clothes she'd picked out for him when her phone vibrated. Pulling it out and looking at the caller ID, she shook her head and answered it.

"Yes, Dad. I know, Dad. Sorry I didn't call, Dad, but it's none of your business, Dad."

"Roxy!" her father's voice replied. "You're involved with a boy who's in the middle of a murder and kidnapping investigation! What are you trying to do to me? I thought I raised you better than this!"

"Neither of us knew about those things when we met, Dad." She sighed. "I'm a big girl now, Daddy. I can take care of myself."

"I've done a little checking on this 'boyfriend' of yours, do you know *what* he is?"

"I know what he *was*, Daddy, and I know what he is *now*."

"You didn't!" Her father's voice sounded rather shocked.

"Daddy," Roxy growled. How could her father even suspect she'd bitten Sean? That was the problem with phones; you always had to talk around certain subjects, you never knew who might be listening. "Are you accusing your only daughter of being an idiot? Because that's what it sounds like to me."

"I'm coming up there." Her father didn't sound as shocked; obviously he'd gotten the hint. The problem was, the last person she wanted meeting Sean right now was her father. He could be overprotective, especially around her boyfriends.

He'd pulled the old 'cleaning the handgun' trick when she'd brought guys home more than once.

"Come tomorrow." She sighed and tried to remember what Sean had told her about his class schedule. "We can talk while he's in class."

"No, I'm coming up now."

"Daddy?" Roxy said in her sweet little girl voice; she knew her father hated it. "This one's different. You pull any of your tricks, and he'll put you through a wall."

"Oh, I doubt *that*," her father growled back.

"And I'll be helping him," Roxy warned with a growl of her own.

"Jimmy tried to put me through a wall; you saw how that worked out!"

"Jimmy was a wimp." Roxy laughed. Jimmy was the buffest cheetah she'd ever seen, well after her father at least.

There was a pause on the phone for a moment.

"Fine," her father sighed, "what time tomorrow?"

"Be here at ten. Call me and we'll figure it out," she told him with a purr.

"I still want to meet him," her father warned.

"You will, eventually, after we've talked."

"Bye, Roxy. Just remember your father loves you."

"And I love you too!" she said and hung up the phone.

"Who do you love?" Sean asked coming up to her and looking a little shocked.

"Daddy called," she grinned, "let's just say he's not exactly happy with his daughter's latest boyfriend, and he hasn't even met him yet." She paused a moment and tapped her chin with a finger. "I think this is a record, even for him."

Sean looked at her, a little worried. "Great, not only do I have some mysterious group of people after me, but now I have your dad to contend with."

Roxy giggled and kissed him. "Yeah, but I'm worth it."

Sean smiled. "Well, yeah. Of course you are."

"So, any ideas for dinner?"

"Um, I really need to study tonight; could we maybe just get some takeout or something?"

Roxy nodded. "Sure, I need to study too." She ran her finger down his chest; he'd definitely put on some more muscle since she'd seen him heading for the shower yesterday morning. He was bulking up rather quickly. "Something other than your anatomy of course!" she added, then giggled as he blushed brightly.

"Let's go pay for all of this." Sean nodded towards the pile of clothing and shoes in the cart. "Then maybe we can spend an hour or two studying anatomy before we take care of school work?"

"You're learning!" Roxy chuckled.

"Well, I do have a good teacher." Sean chuckled back.

They walked out of the mall with two large bags, Sean wearing his watch once again.

"Don't look now," he sighed, "but that guy behind us about twenty feet; does he seem to be paying just a bit too much attention to us?"

"Huh," Roxy said, stopping for a moment to look at one of the shoe displays in a woman's clothing store, but focusing more on the reflection of the people behind them, "Good catch."

"It's those jackets they wear to hide their holsters," Sean said as they started walking again. "It's like a uniform."

"Do you see any others?"

"No, just him." Sean looked hopeful for a moment. "Maybe there aren't any others left?"

"Well, four last night, two at your friend's place, and what, three in the van?"

"Don't forget the one-armed man," Sean pointed out.

"I'm not. But we don't know if he's dead. I'd guess this guy is just following us and helping to set up the next ambush."

"You'd think they'd have learned by now." Sean sighed.

"Oh they have," Roxy said, noticing the two vans screeching to a halt ten feet in front of them, the doors flying open, and men with guns jumping out.

"Run!" she yelled, and turning around, she ran back towards the mall entrance with Sean hot on her heels.

The man who'd been behind them looked surprised, especially when Roxy tripped him as she went by.

Sean stepped on his stomach as the man was falling, driving him to the ground hard and yelling out, "Sorry! Excuse me!" as he jumped off the guy and kept going.

They pushed past the doors quickly, and suddenly it sounded like a major firefight had erupted outside as the glass doors to the mall shattered behind them.

"What the hell?" Sean panted.

"I don't think they're from around here," Roxy yelled back to him.

"What?"

"This is an open carry state. A lot of people outside were packing. They probably figure those guys were terrorists attacking the mall!"

Sean snuck a glance behind him as they went around the corner; there were four guys running after them wearing balaclavas over their heads, thick black sweaters, holding pistols. Then there were three, as an old lady with a Magnum took one of them out.

"Damn!" he swore and would have laughed if he hadn't been running so hard. Roxy ducked down an emergency exit, setting off the alarm; with all the other noise going on, he doubted anyone heard it. They pounded down the corridor, then out the door into the daylight. Roxy grabbed him and they both flattened against the wall behind the door and waited, dropping their shopping bags.

"I think I hear someone," he told her as he caught his breath.

"I can't believe they were this damn stupid!" Roxy replied, shaking her head.

"I'd say they were getting desperate," Sean said, then the door banged open and two men came running out, leading with their guns. One was wounded, and their clothing was shot up, revealing body armor underneath.

Jumping forward, Sean grabbed one from behind, and without even thinking about it, he slammed the man's head into the concrete wall of the mall, cracking his skull and killing him instantly.

Roxy had the other one from behind, and had not only taken his gun, but had it pressed against his head.

"Who are you assholes, and what do you want?" she growled.

"You can't kill us all!" the man gasped, with the same vague accent the other man from last night had had. "Sooner or later, we'll get our hands on it!"

"On what?" Sean asked, coming over and looking the man in the face. There was nothing about him that made him stand out; he looked vaguely European, but then so did a lot of people in Nevada.

"Your father's legacy!" the man exclaimed.

Sean laughed and shook his head. "They took my father's legacy when he died, *all* of it, *everything*! I have nothing left of his, or even mine! Whatever the hell it is you're looking for, either the government got it, or the people he owed money took it!" Sean was all but yelling now.

"And even if he *had* left me anything, I'd have sold it years ago! Do you think I *liked* living in poverty? Buying my clothes from Goodwill? Living in a tiny trailer in a cheap park while all the kids made fun of me because I was poor?

"Just leave me the fuck alone! I don't have anything!"

Sean hauled off and slapped the guy across the face, dropping him.

"Oh shit," Sean said and looked up at Roxy, "I didn't kill him, did I?"

"No, but you sure as hell knocked him out. Let's get our things and go! Last thing I want to do is end up on the news or down at the police station!"

Sean nodded and grabbing his bags, they took off away from the mall, dodging through the neighborhood next to it. They weren't the only ones looking to get away from all the shooting, not that he could hear any more at this point. But what he *could* hear were police sirens as every cop within twenty miles converged on the mall. Two police helicopters quickly shot overhead and started to circle the area.

"So much for a quiet night of making out and studying." Sean sighed as they slowed down to a walk.

"Yeah, here hold this," Roxy said, shoved the other bag at him, and got out her phone.

"Who are you calling?"

"That witch I know." She paused a moment, then said, "Jolene?"

"Oh, *hi* Roxy," Jolene said over the phone, "what are you doing?"

"Walking home. Just what, or should I ask who, are you doing?"

"Oh, nothing that enjoyable I'm afraid, but the news on TV looks rather exciting. Some sort of terror attack on the mall?"

"Yeah, I saw it. I need you to come by my place."

Roxy heard Jolene laugh. "You need me? Isn't it supposed to work the other way around?"

"Just get your ass over to my place, and get it there now, Jolene, understand?"

Jolene paused a second and her voice suddenly sounded a lot less relaxed. "I thought we were friends, Roxy?"

"Why the hell do you think I'm calling you? I need help, please Jolene?"

"I'll be there," Jolene said and hung up.

"Jolene?" Sean asked. "Isn't that your hot girlfriend?"

Roxy sighed and rolled her eyes. "Why does everyone call her that?"

"Because she is?" Sean replied honestly. He'd seen Jolene over at Roxy's quite a few times over the last two years. She looked like Kate Upton with brown hair, only sexier, if such a thing were possible.

"And why does everyone always think we're a thing?" Roxy grumbled.

"Um, because of the noises that come from your room when she's over?" Sean smirked. "I mean, I don't have a problem with two sexy women having some fun, mind you..." Looking up, he noticed Roxy was the brightest shade of red he'd ever seen.

"It's not like that," she mumbled, looking embarrassed.

"It's not?"

"Well, not exactly. It's complicated." Roxy shook her head. "We're getting off track here, I'll explain later."

"I'm going to hold you to that," Sean teased, lowering his voice. "Actually, I think I'm going to hold you against a lot of things!"

"Lions," Roxy grumbled.

"Go put your things away, then come to my room," Roxy told Sean when they got back to the house.

Sean nodded. "Okay. What about dinner?"

"I'll order a couple of pizzas, alright?"

"Sounds good!"

Going into his room, Sean considered just dumping everything on the bed, going over to Roxy's, and abusing that hot little body of hers for a while, but then he'd still have this stuff to put away, and she'd be upset with him for slacking off. Looking bad in her eyes was something he wanted to avoid. Besides, after they finished studying, he'd have all night with her in bed.

She was his now, there was no reason to rush things.

That thought stopped him, and he smiled and shook his head, *that* one didn't sound like it came from his lion. Maybe he was integrating, as she'd called it? He sure hoped so; having arguments with himself in his head was just a little disquieting.

Roxy opened the door and looked at Jolene, who was sitting on her bed wearing a smile and not much else.

"Thanks for coming over," Roxy said, giving Jolene a hug as she stood up to greet her. "Now put some clothes back on. I need you to look at somebody."

Jolene smirked. "Why can't I look at them naked? They a prude or something?"

"Because I don't feel like sharing him just yet, and you've got your work cut out for you."

"Oh! New boyfriend?" Jolene asked and bounced on her toes. The whole effect was rather interesting on Jolene's shapely body; as always, Jolene pretty much emanated sexuality. Roxy wasn't sure how Jolene was going to react to Sean, though she was pretty sure how Sean and his lion would both react.

"Clothing, on now." Roxy pointed, and with a pout Jolene, slipped into her jeans then pulled her top on.

"Yes," Roxy continued, "I have a new boyfriend, he's a lion-were, and if you don't know much about them, I suggest you look it up."

"Aren't lions into prides and harems, and stuff like that?" Jolene asked.

Roxy nodded. "Exactly, and if you don't want to end up in his, you might want to exercise just a little bit of caution."

Jolene laughed. "But I'm not a lycan. Everyone knows lycans and humans don't mate."

"There are always exceptions," Roxy sighed, "and don't be surprised if you become one of them. You've been warned."

Jolene blinked a moment and looked at Roxy. "You serious?"

"All of this is very serious. Someone is after my Sean, and neither one of us has any idea why. So before I start asking people who might know, I thought perhaps you could use your magic on him and find out if there's anything special about him."

"Wait, you just warned me a moment ago that I probably shouldn't sleep with him, and now you're saying you want me to use my magic on him? Roxy, I'm a tantric witch!"

"Yeah, I know," Roxy sighed, "but you're the only person I know I can trust, and I have to start somewhere."

Jolene nodded. "Okay, well tell me what you know, and I'll see what I can do."

Sean knocked, opened the door, and walked into Roxy's room. Roxy was pacing back and forth, talking to her friend Jolene, who was sitting cross-legged on the bed.

Jolene was barefoot, a pair of very racy spike heels on the floor, wearing a pair of jeans and a peasant blouse cut low in the front that did nothing to hide her abundant cleavage. She was more curvy than Roxy was, and Sean figured she was maybe five and a half feet tall, with long brown hair that came down to her very shapely ass.

"...the only thing I can't figure out, is why they haven't attacked here," Roxy was just finishing up. She then turned, smiling at him as he entered and came over, then gave him a hug and a very passionate kiss. Sean wondered if she was perhaps marking her territory in front of her friend.

"Hi, Hon." Roxy sighed.

"Hi, Love," Sean replied, smiling. He could feel his lion preening at the attention, but then, so was he.

"This is my friend Jolene, whom you've mentioned noticing before. Jolene, this is Sean."

"Hi, Sean," Jolene said and rather sensually uncrossed her legs, got up, and came over and gave him a hug. Sean still had one arm around Roxy, but he put the other one around Jolene and hugged her back. She beamed up at him, and damned if he didn't start to get hard.

Letting go of him, Jolene sauntered back over to the bed and sat down. Sean thought he detected a faint growl from Roxy, so he hugged her a little tighter and rubbed up against her.

"Okay," Jolene started, "I think that may be my fault." She looked a little embarrassed.

"Your fault?" Roxy look surprised. "How?"

"I've warded this entire building against scrying and tracking. Magically, this place doesn't exist. So anyone using magical means to locate anyone inside this building," Jolene shrugged and Sean appreciated the way it made her chest bounce, "won't find them when they're here."

"Why did you ward the house?" Sean asked.

"Because of her." Jolene grinned and pointed at Roxy. "I'm over here recharging my batteries often enough that I don't want anyone to know about it."

Sean looked at Roxy, who was now blushing fiercely and squirming against him, then he looked back at Jolene. "Wait, what? Recharging your batteries?"

"I'm a tantric witch, Sean. Do you know what that means?"

"You use sex to cast magic?" Sean blinked and looked at Roxy again. "You've been casting magic in here?"

Jolene laughed. "No, not really. Well, except for when I recharge the wards. You see, I use the power sex gives me to do spells and other magic. Since I can store the power inside me, I just come here to do a little 'recharging'," and she smiled at Roxy so warmly that Sean almost felt jealous.

"Jolene and I became friends back when I first started college here," Roxy spoke up. "She eventually figured out what I was, and told me what she was, and well, we were already friends, and sex with a friend is more powerful than with a stranger, and ah, I sorta agreed to help her out if she'd help me out."

"Ooookay," Sean said and looked at Roxy, then back to Jolene, then back at Roxy, his imagination running wild at this point.

"There's one other thing to it," Jolene added, "that Roxy didn't mention."

"You mean this gets better?" Sean said, grinning, and Roxy smacked him on the butt.

"While I get okay power from having sex with humans, I get a lot more from creatures with a magical potential."

"Like lycans?"

"*Especially* lycans," Jolene said with a wink as she smiled at him.

"Just remember one thing," Roxy growled in his ear softly.

"What?"

"Lycans and humans don't mate. It rarely ever works out."

'What about lycans and witches?' his lion growled rather lustily.

"What about lycans and witches?" Sean repeated with a smirk.

"Just tell your lion not to be in a rush to add her to his pride."

"What about me?" he teased.

Roxy scowled at him, and Jolene laughed from the bed.

"I'm not looking to join any prides, don't worry. I'm far too happy playing the field."

"Sure you are," Sean smiled and nodded. "So, now what?"

"Well, Roxy wants me to use my magic on you to see what I can learn."

"Does that mean we're going to have sex?" Sean asked, a little surprised.

"No!" Roxy growled.

"Probably not," Jolene said with a smile.

Sean shrugged. "Okay, so what do I do?"

"You can start by stripping."

"Umm…" Sean glanced down at the obvious tent in his trousers.

"Don't worry, I've seen lots of erections, and I just love looking at them!" Jolene said and licked her lips, winking at him again. "And I'm sure Roxy will be more than happy to help you with it once this is done."

He looked at Roxy, who'd already started to undo his belt. Grabbing his t-shirt, he pulled it up over his head and tossed it on Roxy's desk as his pants fell down around his ankles. He wasn't wearing any underwear, and he'd left his shoes and socks back in his room. Stepping out of his jeans, he was completely naked.

Jolene looked him up and down. "Wow, I had no idea you were so well developed under those clothes!"

"Don't swell his ego too much!" Roxy chuckled.

"I don't think it could swell any more!" Jolene teased, and Sean blushed just a little. To say he was excited was an understatement.

"Take the watch off, too," Jolene said, noticing it. "Any other jewelry?" She continued looking him over.

"Nope," he said and handed the watch to Roxy, who put it on the table.

"Okay, I need you to lie down on the bed, on your back," she said,taking his hand., She brought him over to the bed and had him lay down on his back. Jolene then positioned his hands, folded, over his navel, then grabbing his feet, she spread his legs apart so his feet were at the same width as his shoulders.

"Okay, close your eyes."

Sean did as she asked, and after a moment, he felt one of her hands on his forehead and the other on his folded hands.

He started to see images. It took him a moment to realize that he was reliving Friday all over again. It seemed to be going well, until the moment he was grabbed from behind.

Then it stopped.

"Shit," Jolene swore.

"What?" Roxy asked, sounding worried.

"There's something going on here. This is going to be a bit harder than I thought."

He felt her hands leave him then, and he heard the rustle of fabric.

"What are you… he heard Roxy say.

"You better take your clothes off too, Hon," he heard Jolene say.

Sean opened his eyes and was just about to ask what was going on, when Jolene straddled his chest, naked.

"I need more contact," she said, smiling down at him, "lift your arms a second."

Sean did as he was bidden, and she moved up until her knees were almost in his armpits, her legs lying along his side.

"Good, put your hands where they were before."

Sean nodded and did so, and she sat down on them. Putting her hands on either side of his face, she ran them up into his hair and leaned forward, her full chest only inches away from his face.

"Close your eyes," Jolene instructed him.

Sean did so and almost gasped as she lay down on top of him, his face now well buried between her plump breasts.

"Okay, let's try this *again*," she purred.

Jolene closed her eyes and started to work her magic. Prying through people's memories was usually child's play, at least when they were willing, and this Sean beneath her was *very* willing. Very willing for other things too, she could tell, but she didn't blame him for that; most men were, and to be honest, he was a pretty impressive specimen. Roxy had finally picked a winner, it seemed.

Settling down into Sean's head, she started his Friday all over again, only this time she started at the moment he'd woken up. Sometimes when you ran into a block, having a little momentum helped.

She didn't linger over anything; she just let it all run at the speed of thought, until she came up to his confrontation with Dean again. Once that had played out, she slowed things down and started to push all her power into his memory; she would not be denied. She didn't like it when she was blocked from something she wanted, and she liked it even less when someone was blocked from something that was theirs.

Jolene hit the first wall when Sean was tasered, his body going rigid for a moment under her as he relived the moment.

"It's okay," she whispered, "it's just a memory; it has no power over you."

She felt his surprise and relived his shock as he tried to figure out what was happening. She felt it when he kicked, but she heard the sound he'd missed, the sound of something growling outside the van, the sound of tearing metal.

Then the crash and the pain as he broke his arm and had his leg ripped open.

Jolene hit the second wall then, as he pulled off the hood and looked around, seeing what was happening around him. The lion-were laying waste to the remaining man, who was shooting him with a damn big gun.

The lion-were said something, but she couldn't hear it. Backing the memory up, she threw even more power at it and ran through it again.

The lion-were called him by name; it was peculiar that such a memory would be blocked.

Then he was unconscious again.

Jolene hit another wall and had to force her way through it with even more power. It was a man, one whom Sean's subconscious immediately identified. A friend, an old family friend. He was talking, but she couldn't hear what he was saying.

Jolene rewound and started it again, pushing more energy into it; still there was no sound, she could see his lips moving, even make out some of the words.

With a growl of her own, she rewound the memory once again, and this time she pushed *all* of her power into it, not holding anything back as she ground her body against Sean, who was panting beneath her.

Jolene heard Sampson warn Sean that 'they' were after him, and that he, Sampson, was dying. That they wanted something his father might have left him. She heard all of it, then Sampson bit Sean, infecting him, changing him. She felt the lion inside him take root as his body healed and, left with no coherent mind to steer it as Sean had passed out from blood loss and shock, the lion ran off and hid until it had made enough sense of Sean's thoughts to gather up his dropped books and return to his room.

"What's going on?" Roxy asked; the concern in her voice was clear to hear.

"There's a block in his mind, blocking the memories." Jolene was panting, she was nearly spent, but she'd broken through all the blocks. Now to see if she could find the source.

"Could it be from shock? From what happened? From getting bit?"

"No," Jolene said, "this is magical. Someone's put something in his mind. Aha!" she crowed as she found it.

"A geas, an old and well-buried one, from over a decade ago I'd guess! Someone doesn't want your Sean to remember certain things, or…" Jolene looked at it further; there was something strange about it, but she wasn't sure what. She didn't have enough power left to figure it out.

But she had a nice strong lycan male on his back beneath her with an erection that wouldn't quit.

"Oh, this is going to be fun!" she said, and sitting back up, she looked at Roxy.

"You're not going to…?" Roxy said, her expression a cross between jealousy and concern.

"He's got something nasty in there, and it's going to take a lot of power to remove it." Jolene smiled. "And guess what I have? Two horny lycans who are just *full* of it."

Reaching back behind her, Jolene raised herself up and, taking Sean's length into her hand, she slid back and guided him into her center, settling down and sighing rather happily as she felt him enter her core. There was a lot of power in this one, a *lot!* Roxy had most certainly picked a winner.

"You can use your hands now, Sean, and anything else you'd like!" Jolene giggled, then motioned to Roxy.

"You can sit down right here in front of me and give Sean something to do with his tongue while we make love!" Jolene panted as she felt her own lust beginning to rise. Sean's hands had a hold of her hips and were starting to stroke her thighs as Roxy straddled him; settling down, Roxy started to kiss Jolene, Roxy's hands coming up to massage Jolene's chest, adding her own inherent power to the mix.

Roxy was a little uncomfortable at first. She'd never had a threesome before in her life, ever. She was usually a greedy lover; she didn't like sharing her partners with anyone.

But Jolene, somehow Jolene had always been different. That first hesitant time she'd agree to let Jolene try and 'feed' off her magical essence, she'd agreed more out of a sense of adventure and daring. But the next time had been because Jolene had not only made her feel incredibly good about herself, but because it had been mind-blowing ecstasy as well. Jolene was a very talented lover, which only made sense when you realized she'd need to be in order to get her power, but the process of passing the power along was also extremely enjoyable.

As soon as Roxy started to kiss Jolene, all hesitation fell away; they were doing this for Sean after all, and if Jolene said it had to be done, well, she trusted Jolene. Besides, Sean was one of the few men who had ever rivaled Jolene's ability to make her toes curl, and right now, he was already well along the way to setting her off.

Putting one hand behind Jolene's head, Roxy pulled her closer into a deeper kiss. If Jolene needed energy to help Sean, she was going to make sure she gave her all she could!

Sean's mind was spinning, and not just because he was in bed with two incredibly hot and loving women, and having amazingly orgasmic sex. He could *feel* Jolene pulling the energy out of his body, and using it to slowly take his mind apart. There was something there, something in it, and she was slowly going after it, piece by piece, tendril by tendril. He could feel that it was old, and he could tell that whoever had put it there hadn't done it for Sean's own good.

It was an exercise in both love and lust, endurance and strength. He made love to Jolene for what seemed like hours, filling her with his essence several times, all while she and Roxy made love above him. Then positions changed, and suddenly he was inside his Roxy, seeking completion with her, with Jolene in a secondary role now, yet she was still deep inside his mind, still tapping the energies of the two of them, but as their beasts met and Sean buried himself in Roxy, their energy spiraled higher and he felt the thing in his mind begin to fade. It lost its power, and slowly, oh so slowly, it disappeared, until suddenly, there was nothing there.

"You can be anything you want to be now, Sean," Jolene's voice filled his mind. "Make your choices from the heart, from your love for Roxy, from the joy of what we've shared here, and all will be well."

Arching up, he emptied himself into Roxy one last time as she cried out in joy with him, then he quickly fell asleep.

"What just happened?" Roxy yawned and watched as Sean all but passed out, obviously exhausted.

Jolene smiled and cuddled up against Roxy. "I removed a rather nasty geas someone put on him. From what I learned in the process, I think it was done to him when his father died."

"What?" Roxy turned to look at Jolene. "Why would anyone do that?"

"Because his father was a powerful wizard, and they didn't want his son to follow in his footsteps?"

"Wait, his father was a wizard?"

Jolene nodded. "That's what I'm guessing. The geas blocked all his magical potential; I'm surprised Sampson was even *able* to infect him. I guess the magic of lycanthropy is different enough, it managed to squeak past the rules.

"But along with the block on his potential, it also blocked his memories. They didn't want him to remember anything about his father or his father's work. When he was attacked, well, that was all related to his father, and his father's work. So the geas immediately went to work to block it."

"How does a spell know something like that?" Roxy asked skeptically.

"It doesn't. Sampson told him it was about his father and his father's work. A geas is based in your own mind; in a way, it uses your own mind against you. So once his mind realized what it was…"

"It triggered the geas."

"Exactly." Jolene yawned and stretched out on the bed. "I don't think I've had a magical workout like this, ever. You two are pretty potent, I must say."

"Well," Roxy yawned as well, "I guess we're not getting any studying done tonight." Looking over at her alarm clock, she gasped. "It's three AM!"

"Yup, wake me in the morning; I think I've earned a battery recharge or two!"

"Jolene, after last night, you might want to be gone before he wakes up. He's a lion, and he's going to start building a pride soon."

"Oh?" Jolene giggled. "Worried about competition?"

Roxy blushed. "Actually, of all the people I could want to be in it with me, you're definitely my first choice."

Now it was Jolene's turn to look surprised.

"Hey," Roxy grinned wearily, "I warned you. I love him, and I can tell he loves me. So of course I'm going to help him get the best women. Besides, it's not like we don't have feelings for each other already, right?"

Supernatural Discoveries

Sean woke up from a deep sleep for one reason only, his bladder was full, and someone was pressing on it. Opening his eyes, he could see it was still dark out; Roxy's clock said five-thirty. Roxy was pressing up against him, her leg drawn up over him, reminding him of his full bladder, while Jolene was curled up against her.

'Want' said his lion as he looked over Jolene's naked body.

"You and me both," Sean whispered to himself. "But first, let's use the bathroom."

It took him a minute to separate himself, then he padded down to the bathroom naked. At this time of night he doubted anyone would be up, and honestly, he really didn't care who saw him naked after the night he'd just had.

Returning to Roxy's room, he spied Sampson's watch on the table, grabbing it he put it on out of habit. It would be just his luck to forget it here, then spend weeks looking for it in his own room.

Climbing back into bed, he snuggled up to Roxy, who murmured in her sleep and rolled over to face Jolene. He tucked Roxy under his chin, draped an arm over the two of them, and quickly fell back asleep.

#   #   #

Sean was sitting at a desk. There were a number of thick leather-bound books on the desk, but the covers were all blank.

"Hello, Sean."

Looking up, Sean saw his father. He was wearing what looked like a chemist's apron, only it had arcane symbols drawn on it. His hair was black, like Sean's, with a slight touch of gray at the temples. He looked concerned, but not too worried.

"Dad? What are you doing here?" he asked, sitting behind the desk, unable to stand.

"If you're seeing this, I'm probably dead. A number of people have begun to take an interest in my work, and not in a good way."

"Is this a recording of some kind?" Sean asked and looked around; he was in a dream state of some kind. Then it came to him, he'd just gone back to sleep with Roxy and Jolene after a rather exhausting marathon of tantric magic to remove something that Jolene said had been bad for him.

"I've enchanted this watch," Sean saw his father hold up the watch that Sampson had given him, "and I've asked Sampson to give it to you on your eighteenth birthday, once you've gotten old enough to understand magic, how it works, and have the energy to use it.

"There are things I want to teach you, but before I can do that, you'll need to learn the basics, and that's the reason for all of this. If the narrow-minded members of the five councils have their way, I'll be barred from continuing my work, perhaps even stripped of any power and cast out of magical society. And if the greedy members of certain circles have *their* way, well, I won't go down without a fight, and I won't give up that which is mine, that which is, of course, now yours.

"I've arranged this spell so that it can only affect you, only be used by you. I have put all my basic spell knowledge and theory into it. Simply by closing your eyes and concentrating, you can come to this place and study these things.

"You'll also be brought here, every night, to study. Do not lose the watch; you must be wearing it for the spell to work. Do not tell others about the watch, lest they try and take it from you, even though it will not work for anyone but you.

"There's one more important thing you must learn first, and you will learn that now. A magic user must decide what parts of his essence he will dedicate to learning a particular spell or characteristic before he can learn it. How fast you will learn it will depend on how hard you work. As you progress in skill and in age, you will have more to spend, but remember to spend wisely. Once spent, you cannot undo what you have done.

"Now, let us begin."

One of the books in front of Sean suddenly lit up and had a title on the cover, 'Mastery of Self'.

Opening it up, he started to read. It told him first about the general aspects of his mind and his body that he could improve, with time. It reminded him very much of the character creation and building process of all the D&D and video games he'd played as a kid. Well, still played, to be honest.

You accumulated energy over time and through study. The type of energy you accumulated often determined how it must be spent, but there was a certain amount of wiggle room on some of the topics.

So some things and some changes could be made quickly, while others would take more time and effort. Some would require him to return and spend more of his energy; he liked to think of it as 'points', since it was always in the same discrete 'packets' or amounts, over time.

Once how it worked was explained, the spell appeared in the book, and it took him only a moment to learn it.

He cast it.

He blinked in surprise as he looked it over. The similarities between it and several of his favorite games were so great, he wondered if those games had originally been designed by magic users to help teach their children through play.

Either that, or someone had decided to make a killing in the gaming market by simply pirating the actual system in use today.

First there were his physical stats, and looking at them, he was shocked to see how high they were, after what he'd read to be average range in the book. Apparently his lycanthropy had given him a huge advantage there.

Second there were his mental stats, and some of them were slightly above average; he suspected that his time in college had raised them.

The third set of stats was labeled magical. They were also higher than expected, quite a bit higher, but he had no clue at all as to why that would be.

Then he looked at his points available in each of the three categories: physical, mental, magical, and something called 'scholarly' that wasn't apparently a stat, and even though it was a dream, his jaw still dropped.

He quickly went back and looked at the book, jumping back and forth between it and his skills chart several times. It was annoying that he couldn't look at them side by side, but he started looking at each of the categories and tried to figure out why his numbers were so different from the examples given in the book.

It looked like a lot of the physical points had already been spent due to his lycanthropy, which he suddenly suspected had gotten him more than a few 'bonus' points. In each of the first three skills, constitution, agility, and strength, his numbers were well beyond anything the book mentioned, and while agility was supposed to be a 'locked' skill like constitution was, it looked like he could still put points into it.

That was interesting.

Then there was a box at the bottom of the list labeled 'regeneration'; that wasn't even in the book! But it sounded good, so he stuck a couple more levels into that, which turned out not to be cheap. Based on what he'd learned from the games he'd played in the past, he pushed most of the remaining points into agility, and left himself a couple extra, just in case. His strength was already beyond that of a human, so he'd hold off before adding any more there.

Under mental, there were five categories; intelligence, wisdom, reasoning, memory, and integration. Again, the last one, integration, wasn't in the book, but obviously had to do with his lycanthropy. The first two in this group were also 'locked', but in a different way. You couldn't put anything into them, but the book said they would increase on their own, as a result of your own work.

So the work he'd done trying to learn to be a better student and to study harder, along with his years in college, had apparently given him some increases in his intelligence, if he was reading this correctly. However, his wisdom increases seem to have come from a life spent scraping to get by, and playing D&D with his friends.

He found that last bit to be amusing, but the real surprise was that his years in college had left him with quite a few points to spend.

Sean looked at the last skill on the list, the one that wasn't in the book, integration. The idea that he could now actually do something to speed up learning to work with his beast, his lion, was pretty damn appealing. He dropped two levels worth of points into it, which was half of what he had left; apparently the lycan skills had a higher point cost per level. That done, he put a couple levels into memory and reasoning as well, and sat on the last two points for later.

There were only three magical stats, ability, mana, and will. Ability was locked and apparently inherited, according to the book, so his being high was probably because of his dad. His mana levels, however, were higher than normal, by quite a bit. Jolene had mentioned several times tonight that lycans had higher energy levels, so maybe that was the reason for it. Only Sean's 'will' stat looked normal, if at the high end of the range.

So he stuck a few points in mana, just because he could, but put all the rest into will. It looked like your will was what drove your ability to cast, so it was probably the most important stat on the entire sheet if you were a magic user.

Skipping back to the book for a minute seemed to confirm that thought.

Done with the 'Stats' part of the sheet, Sean came to what was labeled as scholarly. He had fifty points! He'd been accruing them for almost three years now, and of course hadn't spent a one. Again, his studies had helped a lot in gaining him more points. Apparently studying logic and science had helped him quite a bit, as well as his age. The book said you normally started with somewhere between six or eight depending on your schooling until that point.

Running down the lists of spells, he quickly realized one thing; his father had obviously been an alchemist. There were other things there; some of them were strange, and some of them didn't look all that good, either. If his father had learned some of those, he could see why perhaps his dad wasn't as popular with some people as you might expect.

He'd have to think about all of this. A few of the spells stood out almost instantly, like healing, protection from spells, and some shield spells. Then there was a list of offensive spells, as well as a number of ones he couldn't make head nor tails of right now.

He decided it could all wait until morning. He was tired.

Taking another look around the room, he saw a sign that said exit, and as he thought about using it, he left the dream and went back to sleep.

Monday, Monday

Sean woke up when the alarm went off, but Roxy and Jolene were both still soundly asleep. With a little coaxing using lips, teeth, and fingers, Roxy woke up fairly quickly, and went from grumpy to sighing, then moaning happily in short order. By the time he was done with her, Jolene had woken up and was demanding 'her fair share' for all the work she'd done last night.

Roxy kicked them both out of her room when she got back from the shower; she'd remembered her father was going to show up sometime this morning, and she had class. Sean realized he had class as well, but decided missing one wouldn't hurt, and being with Jolene was a lot more fun.

"So, just how does magic work?" he asked her later, when they were lying in his bed together covered in sweat.

"That's a question that would take years to answer." Jolene sighed, cuddling up against him. Sean had replaced a lot of her power this morning. She'd actually woken up because of the power Sean and Roxy had been giving off while having sex, not because they'd been all that noisy.

"Doesn't anyone know?"

"Oh, people know, but it's different for every type of magic. A lot of mine is mentally based, like you saw last night. I have to be touching someone to affect them. The spells I have, where I don't have to be touching someone or something, require certain sounds to be uttered while making certain gestures. Most of which are really just mnemonic keys to my own mind to help shape and focus the magical energy, or what most folks call mana, in my body."

"And how do you learn spells?"

"Well, some I studied. I had a master who taught me a bunch of basic spells, then he taught me what he claimed was his greatest secret," Jolene said with a wink.

"And that was?" Sean asked her.

Jolene laughed. "Why would I tell you his greatest secret?"

Sean rolled over on top of her and, pinning her hands above her head with one hand, he started to tickle her with the other.

"No fair!" Jolene laughed.

"Hey, you shouldn't have told me if you weren't going to come clean!" Sean laughed. "Besides, who else can you brag too?"

"Okay! Okay, I give!"

Sean stopped and gave her a nice long kiss until she got all soft and cuddly under him.

"So, you were saying?"

"Hmmm? About what?" Jolene grinned.

"I can either tickle you, or we can do other things," he growled.

"Other things?"

"Fun things," Sean said lowering his voice even more.

"Oh, I like the sound of that!" Jolene said in a sultry voice of her own.

"So, what is this secret?"

"Oh, I just make them up."

Sean blinked at her, "What?"

"I make them up as I go. You see, tantric magic is pretty flexible. Well, at least as flexible as the caster. I've got all the basics down pat, and when I have, say, a very handsome lion and a very sexy cheetah to work with, and I can throw all the energy I want at a problem, well then, I just brute force my way through it until I find what I want. Then I look at what I've learned and use my finesse."

"I got a bunch of lists and books I need to go through." Sean sighed and rolled off her on and back onto his side.

"Where?" Jolene asked, looking around the room.

"In my head," he said, tapping his temple. "Apparently whatever you got rid of had been blocking some sort of teaching spell my dad had put on me that was supposed to activate when I turned eighteen."

"Wow, I've heard of those, from a few young wizards I met a few years back. They told me they have this form-like thing that they have to use to progress into anything new."

"Oh? They mention anything else?"

"Well, you can study anything you want to, really, though most families tend to follow certain paths in their studies. All they can do is learn spells with it though, which is kind of sad. I can use my magic on myself, my body, to help keep healthy and in shape."

"I can use it on my physical abilities, my 'stats', if you will," Sean admitted.

"That sounds different," Jolene said slowly, after thinking about it a moment. "You might want to talk to some other wizards or magic users to see if it's the same for them."

"Right now, I'd rather keep a low profile," Sean confessed. "I've already got one set of enemies out there, and if that spell was blocking my abilities, who knows who else will be unhappy to hear it's gone."

Jolene's eyes widened a bit when he said that. "Or that there's a lycan who can practice wizard magic!"

"Aren't there any lycan magic users?"

Jolene shrugged, and Sean leaned over to kiss one of her breasts as her movement made it jiggle. "Minor ones, simple alchemists, lay healers, hedge wizards. Ooo, that felt good, do that again."

Sean was more than happy to comply.

"Also, lycans are looked down upon by most magic users and the greater magical community."

"Why?" Sean asked, then gave her a little nip that made her gasp.

"Because you're animals, of course."

"Animals?" Sean growled and gave her another, harder, nip, enjoying the way she arched her back and moaned.

"Oh, they have a low opinion of tantric magic users too; they say we're all sluts and whores."

"They sound pretty stuck up then, if you ask me."

"And if your father's best friend was a werelion, he probably already had a strike against him." Jolene moaned and started putting her own hands to good use.

"Time to pay up, kitty cat," she said and shivered as he nibbled at her nipples again.

"With pleasure!" Sean teased.

"Oh, yes. With lots of pleasure!"

It was noon by the time he got out of the shower and dressed, so grabbing his meal plan tickets, Sean headed down to the college cafeteria while keeping a wary eye on his surroundings. He noticed there were a lot more cops on campus today, and campus security was being very visible.

Piling his tray high with food, he found a quiet corner to sit in with his back to the wall so he could observe all of the comings and goings.

"Sean!"

He looked up and saw Alex, who had his own lunch and was heading over to where he was sitting.

"Oh, hey Alex, what's up?"

"I didn't see you in classes this morning; I was wondering if you got caught up in all that shit that went down at the mall yesterday."

"Eh, I decided to sleep in, had a very late night last night." Sean shrugged.

"Stayed up late playing with your new girlfriend?" Alex joked.

Sean nodded and looked around the room; no one was paying them any attention. "Yeah, that was most of it. After everything that's gone on this weekend, I think I needed a break."

"My mom told me Mrs. Grady said the cops were at your mom's place yesterday? And that they blocked off your neighbor's house?"

Sean sighed; how the hell he'd managed to forget about all that, even for a few hours, was beyond him.

"That didn't sound good," Alex said as Sean set down his fork.

"Sampson was found shot to death on Saturday. My mom's missing, no one knows where she is, and someone absolutely trashed our place. Sampson must have caught them in his place, because not only was it trashed, but there were two dead bodies in it."

"Holy shit, man!" Alex gaped. "How are you even here today?"

Sean shrugged. "Not much I can do, and where else can I go? Other than my girlfriend and you guys, I don't have anybody."

"Wow, that's just the worst, man. Here I thought the big excitement was that terrorist attack over at the mall yesterday. Boy did those suckers walk into it, only way it could have been worse was if they had picked a mall in Texas!"

Sean smiled a little wanly at that. "How many people got killed?"

"Five people were shot; two are in critical condition, but the terrorists? I think it's six dead, two in comas, and a couple more who got shot up pretty good."

Sean shook his head, "Roxy and I were shopping when it started; we ran out the back, came home, and decided life was better in bed for the rest of the night."

"Damn, Dude! Talk about a bad day!" Alex commiserated, "You went from one bad thing right into the next!"

"Yeah, so what did I miss at game night Saturday?"

"Zack's monk got killed." Alex grinned, more than happy to change the subject to something a bit less of a downer.

"Again?"

"Yup! That makes the sixth time. John and I are trying to get him to start a new character.

Bringing him back is gonna be hella expensive this time."

Sean snorted. "Yeah, but who else has a kamikaze hobbit monk in their group? Was it as funny as the last time?"

"Oh yeah, you should have been there. He had us all in stitches. Even Chad lost it at one point and couldn't run the game for like fifteen minutes!"

Sean shook his head and chuckled; just a few days ago life had been so damn simple. Go to school, study, play games with his friends.

'You got Roxy, and Jolene soon too,' his lion pointed out, surprising him. Sean had even forgotten about him. But now that he remembered, he realized his lion felt a lot more, well, *there*. He kinda liked it.

"So, you going to classes this afternoon?" Alex asked, starting in on his food.

"Yeah," Sean agreed and went back to eating as well, he was starving, and he'd already gone through half of what he'd bought. Classes were a good idea, he knew everyone who belonged in them, and anyone who didn't belong in the building would stand out like a sore thumb.

Plus, sitting in class, maybe he could forget all about his troubles for a few hours more.

Roxy smiled at her father. They were sitting in the back of the same Denny's she and Sean had had lunch in yesterday, and while her father wasn't in uniform, the haircut, clothes, and whole demeanor just screamed 'COP' to everyone in the place.

"Okay," he started, "tell me about him."

"Why?" Roxy grinned. "So you can tell me how I'm wrong and how you know everything about him? Come on, Dad. I *know* you've had everyone in the department searching all the records for every little scrap of information on him. So let's just cut to the chase, and you can tell me how bad he is for me, and why."

"Honey, I'm hurt that you'd even say that!" her father protested, looking the very picture of wounded innocence.

"Save it for the judge, Dad!" Roxy laughed. "I stopped falling for that when I was thirteen!"

"Honey, I'm your father, it's my *job* to look out for you."

"Uh huh, sure, fine. But your little girl is all grown up now, Daddy. You *know* I can take care of myself, *you* taught me after all."

"Still, this could be dangerous, Honey."

"Oh? Any more dangerous than being the Sheriff's only daughter?" Roxy looked up at her father and shook her head. "You know, I used to be really mad at you for that time Paulson and his men grabbed me to try and pressure you. Now? I'm glad it happened, because it taught me how to deal with those kinds of people."

Roxy had the pleasure of watching her father stiffen for a moment. The Paulson gang hadn't realized that things like lycans existed. After she'd finished with them, they were no longer able to care.

"I'm sorry about that, Honey, really, I…"

Roxy waved her hand, cutting her father off, "Water under the bridge, Dad. I'm not letting go of this one. Someone threw him in the deep end and thank god I was there to keep him from drowning."

"There's going to be trouble, Honey, I can smell it."

"There's already been trouble, Daddy. He's mine."

"You've only known him since what, Saturday? How can he be *yours* already?"

Roxy shrugged and grinned, "He's a lion, he laid claim to me pretty damn quick; I don't think he even realized he'd done it. He'd only been bitten the night before."

"He's been a lion less than a day, and you're already hooking up for life with him?" The disbelief on her father's face was palpable.

"Well, first off, I've known Sean for years, but he wasn't one of us, so I never really pursued anything with him. So it's not like I didn't know him, and Dad, really, *he's a lion!* Trust me on this one, Dad. The guy that bit him helped raise him, Sean's got his head screwed on right, and while you may be my father and all that, if you laid a finger on me in front of him, he'd probably rip your arm off and beat you to death with it.

"He's got a pretty serious thing for me."

Her father sighed, conceding defeat. "Yeah, lions are like that. They fill their prides with kick-ass women and then go absolutely mental if anyone even looks at them sideways." His daughter was the most headstrong of all his kids; his wife Gloria said Roxy took after him too much. He guessed he shouldn't be surprised that a lion would snag her.

"So who was the lion?"

"His neighbor, Sampson," Roxy told him.

"The dead guy?"

"I guess I better tell you what I know," Roxy sighed, "and this is family now, Dad, got that?"

Her father nodded; being a sheriff was one thing, but when you were a lycan, family obviously came first.

Thirty minutes later, Bill Channing was wondering if he could hit his daughter over the head, stuff her in the back of the car, and lock her up back home.

"What have you gotten yourself into, Roxy?"

Roxy smiled winningly at her father. "That, Daddy, is what I want *you* to find out."

Her father shook his head. "You know the different councils that oversee the wizards and other magic users don't care much for us, Honey. They're not going to want to tell me anything about Sean's father, and this sounds exactly like the kind of screwed up mess they'd cause with their politicking."

"It's been over a decade; people aren't good with secrets, I'm sure somebody has talked, or is willing to talk. Besides, isn't secrecy supposed to be some big thing with those guys?" Roxy pointed out. "With that attack yesterday, they definitely drew a lot of attention. You could just tell them that, once again, the lycans are trying to cover up their mistakes.

"I mean really, Dad, didn't you tell me they're always trying to get you to cover up their dirty work for them?"

He nodded slowly and sighed. "Well, the governor did call me this morning, wants to set up a task force, and as Vegas gets the lion's share of the state budget," her father almost winced as he said it, "the governor figures we probably have some experts on staff to help him. I'll set Kenneth on it. That'll give me a line on things."

"How's Kenny doing?" Roxy asked.

"He's going to be crushed when he finds out you're off the market."

Roxy made a face. "Sure he is. Rebecca told me he's all but moved into her place."

Her father laughed. "I still think he'll be crushed. So when do I get to meet this Sean?"

"My Sean," Roxy corrected.

"Okay, *your* Sean."

Roxy got out her phone and sent Sean a text to see when he'd be free to meet her and her dad.

She got a reply almost immediately.

"His last class gets out at three," she said. It was already after one.

"He's got people hunting him, and he's still going to classes?" Her dad had to laugh at that. "Either he's really ballsy, or he's really stupid."

"Or maybe he's just really smart." Roxy smirked. "The campus is crawling with cops today, and you can't just walk into a classroom if you're not a student. Everyone knows everyone else there, Dad."

Her father nodded and conceded the point. It did make sense.

"Well, come on, let's go shopping," her father said, signaling for the bill.

"I don't need another pistol, Dad. I already have two."

"Maybe your boyfriend might like one?"

"He's only twenty; he can't carry concealed yet."

"When's his birthday?"

Roxy shrugged. "I haven't asked him yet.

"March twenty-third." Her father grinned.

Roxy sighed. "I should have figured." She sat up suddenly, "That's…"

"A week and a half away," he finished.

"No, it's in the middle of Spring Break! I'd forgotten all about Spring Break! I need to cancel my plans!"

Her father blinked. "Plans?"

Roxy smirked at her dad. "I usually go to Daytona with all the other gals and engage in a week of drunken debauchery. You know, like your sons, my brothers, do?"

"Maybe you should just take Sean with you? Get out of town for a little while?"

Roxy nodded. "Yeah, but I don't think a beach in Florida surrounded by a million drunk kids is the place for that."

"Uh huh," her dad said as he took the check from the waitress and, after looking at it, threw a bunch of bills down on the table to cover everything.

"Let's go, I'm sure we can find something you think he might like."

Roxy sighed and grinned, her dad loved to shop for guns whenever he was upset about something. Considering all the things she and her brothers had put him through, there was quite an arsenal in the family home.

Father in Laws

Sean's first impression of Roxy's father, Bill Channing, was that he was a big man. That lasted for maybe a second as his lion whispered in his head that he, Sean, was bigger. And just like that, all his fears, worries, and concerns went right out the window.

It felt, different. Yeah, it was strange; Sean had never been one to stand up and stand out. He had always kept his head down, like his mother had constantly told him, but then again, he'd always remembered the one rule Sampson had told him, which was the most important he claimed in life: Don't Back Down.

Ever.

Standing there, shaking hands with Roxy's dad, a man who looked like he'd earned his job the hard way, who was big, imposing, and looking at Sean the way fathers all through time had probably looked at their little girls' boyfriends, Sean just smiled. Sean had weighed himself this morning; he'd gained over twenty pounds since the last time he'd done so, and he was starting to look strong, ripped. Just like Sampson had always looked.

"So you're my daughter's latest?" Bill Channing said to Sean as they shook hands.

"No, I'm her *last*," Sean said, still smiling.

Her father scowled at him for a moment, then sighed. "Well, at least you don't scare easily."

Roxy interrupted, "Okay, Dad, Sean, enough of the dominance displays, let's go eat."

"Yes, Honey," Mr. Channing said

"Yes, Love," Sean replied, earning a look from her father.

Sean earned another look when he dragged Roxy into the backseat of the car with him and smiled at her father in the mirror.

"Are you trying to push me, Son?" Mr. Channing said, as he put the car in gear and drove off.

Roxy started to say something, but Sean held up his hand, stopping her.

"Actually," Sean said, "my dad died when I was eight, and suddenly, after all these years, I just got a new one. Roxy thinks the world of you, and I can see why."

Sean watched as Roxy's dad seemed to deflate a little, then grumbled as Roxy leaned over and kissed Sean.

"Just what I need, another wiseass son," Mr. Channing grumbled.

Roxy laughed. "You raised four of them, Dad, so you sure must like them!"

Sean relaxed back into the seat and, for the moment, everything seemed normal and right with the world.

"We're being followed," Roxy said five minutes later, and Sean sighed and sat up.

"Yeah, I had a few of the boys from the local PD assigned to follow me around in an unmarked car today," Mr. Channing said as he turned into the parking lot for a rather pricey steakhouse.

"Why'd you do that?" Sean asked.

"Because with all of the trouble you two seem to have been drawing lately, I thought it might be a good idea."

"I was kind of hoping that after yesterday, they would have backed off for a while."

"If they were smart enough to do that, they'd never have tried what they did at the mall," Mr. Channing pointed out. "Though something like that had to have sucked up a lot of resources, in which case things should quiet down for a little while."

Sean nodded. They parked without further harassment and were quickly seated at a nice table in the back. It was still a little while before the dinner rush.

Sean made sure to order a lot of food this time, and dinner passed rather nicely with pleasant small talk about the Channing family, and what Roxy's brothers were all up to.

Dinner finished, they were eating dessert when Mr. Channing brought the conversation back to the present.

"So, Sean, what do you know about your father?"

Sean shook his head. "Not much, really. I know now he was a pretty accomplished alchemist, and apparently he was doing things that some people didn't approve of, while others wanted to get their hands on it."

"What?!" Roxy said, looking at him.

Sean blushed and turned to face her. "I'm sorry, Hon. After Jolene removed that, spell or thing on me…"

"Geas," Roxy filled in.

"I had a dream. Apparently my father had set a bunch of training spells and such on me before he died. Well, they activated last night, and I didn't get the chance to tell you before you left for class."

Roxy calmed down and patted his leg under the table. Jolene had been doing her best to distract him this morning, after he'd already seriously distracted her beforehand.

"So, does this mean you're an alchemist too?" Mr. Channing asked.

Sean shrugged. "I have all the stuff he wanted me to study in my head now, but I haven't even begun to start on it. I still have a year of college left, and well, I don't have clue one as to where to start with all of this.

"Right now, I'd just like to find out who the hell is after me, why they're after me, and make them stop," Sean growled out the last bit, or rather, Sean and his lion did; they were a lot more in tune today.

"Well, I pulled all the records I could on your father yesterday. A lot of them have been archived; he's been dead for twelve years now, after all. But what was done to you and your mom, well that was a big red flag. A lot of people dumped a lot of crap on the two of you.

"None of that makes any sense. I don't recall hearing anything about it down in Vegas, and Sid, the guy who's sheriff here now, he wasn't living in Reno back then, so he doesn't know anything about it either."

"We tried asking one of them," Sean admitted, looking down at his plate. "He seemed to think I had some legacy of my dad's." Sean shook his head. "We were cleaned out, completely. The few things they left us I know they went over and let us have only because they weren't worth much." Sean looked up at Mr. Channing. "And now that I know that they cast some nasty spell on me when I was still just a child, I know there's no way my father could have left me anything. They're just grasping at straws for something that doesn't exist anymore, if it ever did."

Sean watched as Mr. Channing sat back and thought about it, obviously mulling it over.

"Okay," Mr. Channing said after a couple of minutes of silence, "here's what I suggest: drop out of college and disappear for a while. Study as much of the stuff your father left you as you can. Alchemists make good money; there aren't a lot of them around. I'll dig into your father's background as much as I can, and I'll use some of my own connections to see if I can make these assholes go away. If not, I know some people who sure as hell can."

Sean blinked. "Drop out? I'm more than halfway through the semester!"

"We're pretty sure they're using magical means to track him, Dad," Roxy piped up. "So it doesn't matter where we go, they're still gonna find us."

"But wouldn't you rather be someplace where you can see them coming?" Mr. Channing replied to his daughter.

"Actually," Sean said, "I grew up here; I've worked damn near every place around here. These guys, they stand out. I think I can see them a lot better here, and there's a lot more places to lose them."

"They already grabbed you once," Mr. Channing pointed out.

"Yeah, but I'm not that kid anymore. Anyone who tries to grab me now isn't going to live to regret it," Sean growled in a low voice.

Mr. Channing nodded slowly. "Well, every man has to make his own decision on when and where he's going to stand his ground. You take care of my daughter, you hear? Anything happens to her, and I'm going to be *pissed*."

When they got back out to the car, Mr. Channing opened the trunk and waved Sean over as Roxy got in the back.

"You know how to handle and shoot a pistol?" Mr. Channing asked Sean.

Sean rolled his eyes. "This is Reno, kinda hard not to learn how to shoot around here."

"Don't get wise, have you had any training?"

Sean nodded. "Yeah, Sampson trained me."

"My daughter said he was some sort of soldier?"

"Yeah, he was. He taught me how to shoot and everything. But I never had the money to buy a gun. Not like I had anything to steal."

Mr. Channing pulled out a box and handed it to Sean.

"Consider this a mating gift. My daughter has made it pretty clear you two are in this for the long haul."

"Thanks?" Sean said a little unsure. "But we can't open carry on campus."

"Your CCW is in the box."

"What? I'm not even twenty-one yet."

"No, but you will be soon. Sid owed me a few favors, and well, there exceptions to every rule. The holsters I got you are all elastic, so you can shift in them. Figure out which one you like and start packing. Claws are nice, but you can't kill someone from the other side of a parking lot with them."

Sean nodded. "What about Roxy?"

"Oh, I took care of her already." Mr. Channing smiled.

"Thanks," Sean smiled, "Dad."

"Just don't make me regret it," Mr. Channing warned in a whisper.

"Well, that went well." Sean sighed, smiling down at Roxy as they laid on her bed. The very first thing they'd done after closing the door was to shed their clothes, get on the bed, and screw their brains out.

Roxy smiled and kissed him. "I think he likes you."

"Of course he does!" Sean grinned. "Everyone likes me!"

"Uh huh, suuuure," Roxy drawled. "So, aren't you going to open up your present and see what my dad got you?"

"The box is heavy enough; I'm guessing a fifty-caliber Desert Eagle?"

Roxy laughed. "Right gun, wrong caliber. It's a forty-four Magnum. He figures your hybrid hands have got to be pretty big, so you might not be able to use a smaller gun. And forty-four is a lot cheaper than fifty."

Sean nodded, then frowned.

"What?"

"Who knows when I'll be able to achieve my hybrid form."

"Yes, well, I have to study, and you probably should too. Why not try doing it as a lion?"

Sean laughed, then stopped when he saw she was serious.

"You're not kidding, are you?" he asked.

"It works, trust me. I did it all through sixth grade because I wanted to get to my hybrid form before any of my friends."

"I thought being born a lycan, you got that automatically?"

"Nope, we have to work at it just like anyone else. We just get the advantage of having years to get used to our animal. Though it's no fun going through puberty as a lycan, trust me on that!"

"What do you think of your father's suggestion that I drop out of college?"

Roxy sighed. "Honestly, I don't know, Hon. I guess it depends on how you do with learning the other stuff. He might be right about pursuing the alchemy thing, but then again, what do *you* want to do?"

Sean shook his head. "I haven't even started to look at any of the spells or figure out what it takes to learn them. And the way the whole thing works is just weird. It's like an RPG, I'm supposed to put 'points' into something I want to learn, and then I can learn it?"

"What did Jolene say? You did ask her, right?"

"She said it's different for different types of magic users, which makes sense. She also said that magic users are stuck-up bigots and they probably won't care much for a lycan who can do magic."

"Well, Dear, we can cross that bridge and blow it up or burn it down when we come to it!" Roxy said with a smile.

Sean gave her another kiss. "Well, I'd better get back to my room and let you study.

"Though you know, we could save a bunch on rent if we shared a room," he added with a wink.

"You do have a point," Roxy grinned and rubbed his head, "and your hair hides it so well!"

"Ha ha," Sean said and carefully got up. Putting on his pants, he grabbed the rest of his clothes and his gift, and went back to his room.

He spent a few minutes going through everything in the box. The permit he stuck in his wallet for now. There was a leg holster, which would probably work with his hybrid form, if it was as big as Sampson's had been. There was a shoulder holster that he could wear under some of his looser shirts and maybe even get away with it.

He could wear a light vest, which would cover it easily; he usually wore one on the cooler days anyway. But he wasn't sure he needed to start carrying a gun just yet. He'd never shot this one, and the last thing he wanted to do was miss what he was shooting at and hit someone else.

Putting the trigger lock on it, he stashed it behind a few textbooks; he could play with it later.

Then putting the books he needed to study on his desk, he took off his pants and *shifted*.

'That was easy,' he thought to himself.

'We're getting better at this; perhaps that thing in your head helps?' was his lion's response.

'I hope so. Well, let's study.'

'I'd rather go out and run around for a while.'

'I don't want Roxy mad at me, do you?'

'I'm sure we could...'

'No, just stop right there. She said this will help us, so we're doing it. As for running around, once it's late, real late. Like after midnight.'

'Promise?'

'I like the idea too, you know,' Sean admitted to himself. He wondered if these conversations would continue, or go away once he mastered this part of himself. He honestly had no idea what he preferred.

'Okay, let's get started!'

One thing Roxy hadn't told him, and which he should have guessed, was that turning pages with paws was *hard!* He'd also put more than one hole through a page, and ripped one in half completely, when he'd tried to use a claw. If nothing else, this was teaching him a whole lot about manual dexterity. Reading as a lion was a bit difficult, as well. He found he was easily distracted, and had a hard time remembering stuff at first.

Part of that was because his lion found it all very boring, so he had to constantly work to get him to pay attention. At least his lion wasn't resisting him at all; otherwise he probably wouldn't be able to do it. But it was slow going.

When Roxy showed up at ten PM with a couple of pizzas, he quickly scarfed them down, and looking at him in his lion form, she shifted into her cheetah form.

"Wow, I had no idea you were so small!" Sean rumbled.

"That's just 'cause *you're* so big," she replied in a higher pitched voice than he was used to hearing from her.

"Am I really that big?" he asked, shaking his mane a bit.

Roxy ducked her head in a nod. "I've seen some weretigers, they can be pretty big, too. But I've never seen a werelion other than you, so I don't really have anything to compare it to."

"I was thinking of going outside and running around for a bit after midnight, interested?"

Roxy shook her head. "I'm going to bed here pretty soon. Unlike you, I didn't get to sleep in."

"Jolene was here, what makes you think I got to sleep?" Sean laughed.

Roxy whacked him in the nose with her tail, hopped up onto his bed, and settled down. Sean got up on it much more carefully – he was afraid if he hopped on it, he'd break it – and cuddled with her for a while.

'What?' he asked as he suddenly woke up, and found his lion feeling excited.

'Let's go outside for a run!'

Sean *'oh'*d to himself and remembered he'd promised; besides, the idea sounded like fun to him.

Carefully stepping off the bed so as to not wake Roxy, he made his way over to the window and looked down.

'Can we make that?' he asked.

'Easily!'

And with that, his lion launched them out the window and down to the ground.

They hit front paws first, then his butt came down and thumped as well, spreading the shock out. It stung a little bit, but he suddenly remembered that he regenerated because he was a werelion. Heck, he'd been shot, and he'd gotten over it so quickly he'd completely forgotten about it until now!

'Let's be careful, last thing we need is our picture in the paper.'

He felt his lion agree with that, and they spent about half an hour prowling around the house. Then they leaped over the fence into one of the neighbor's yards – not one that had a dog of course – and spent a few minutes examining it, then started to work his way towards San Rafael Park. This time of night, he figured it would be nice and empty, and he could run a bit and stretch out his muscles.

Having to cross the campus made it a bit of a challenge, but that just added to the fun, he figured.

Cutting around the north end of the stadium, he made it to the park without seeing anyone, or anyone seeing him.

But on the way back he ran into a problem; he'd just crossed Sierra and was running past the back of some apartment complex when he heard someone exclaim, "Jeff! Come quick! I just saw a lion!"

Ducking into cover, Sean swore, he wasn't in the best place to hide, and someone from the hotel next door had their car lights on. It wasn't enough to show him clearly, but more than enough to give his outline if he moved.

"What are you going on about, Nancy?" he heard.

"A lion! I saw one! I'm sure it was! We better call the police!"

"Nancy, put the phone down. With all the crap going on around here this weekend, I'm sure they don't need reports of a 'lion' running around."

"I know what I saw, Jeff!"

That was all Sean needed, to have a bunch of cops running around. There was no way he'd be able to hide from them. Shifting back to human form, he just started to jog through the brush.

"Look! There it…"

"That's a man, Nancy! I told you, there aren't any lions around here."

"Maybe he's being chased! I tell you I saw a lion!"

Sean cupped his hands around his mouth. "Roar! I'm a lion!" he yelled.

There was a moment's silence, then the sound of someone sputtering, followed by a man laughing.

Sean sighed, and hoped no one could see he was naked; the last thing he needed was the police to be called for *that!* He quickly ran across the Carson-Reno highway and onto campus, it was a bit cold to be running around at night in the altogether. Backtracking the way he'd come, he stopped for a minute and shifted back to his lion form, then padded off at a more sedate pace.

Just as a car came screeching on to campus and headed for the place he'd stopped to change.

'Well that's curious' he thought.

'Let's check it out,' his lion said.

'Sure.'

Ducking around the ticket booths, he leaped up onto the top of them, hunkered down behind the Wolf Pack sign, and peeked down through one of the cutouts to watch what happened.

The car stopped. "Which way?" he heard someone ask.

"I don't know, he disappeared!" a second voice said.

"What do you mean, he disappeared?" the first once asked again.

"Just that, one moment the spell was telling me where he was, and the next it isn't."

"What are you, a hedge wizard? Can't you find a freaking kid?"

"Something's interfering with the spell, I tell you! But he's around here somewhere, so why don't you get off your asses and go look!"

"What if we run into those other guys? Hell, what if we run into the campus police?" a third voice spoke up.

"Then laugh and run away like a bunch of stupid college kids!" the second one said again.

'Curious,' was all Sean could think.

'They're tracking us somehow, I don't like it.'

'I'm open to suggestions,' Sean replied as all four doors opened, and four men piled out of the car. It was dark, but that didn't hamper Sean in the slightest. Three of them started over towards the stadium, splitting up to check the doors.

"Spread out; he's got to be around here somewhere," the one by the car, the second voice, said as he got back in the passenger's seat, sat down, and closed the door. "I'll tell you if he shows up again!"

'A running car with an open door,' Sean thought. *'Think we can sneak down there and steal it?'*

'Just watch me!' His lion chuckled. Standing up, he leapt off of the roof and ducked down under

the bleachers, moving quickly. He shifted back for a moment, and Sean could clearly hear the guy in the car call, "South! South! Under the bleachers!"

Sean shifted back then, and his lion went west, leaping over the low fence and dashing into the shadows. You'd think a huge four-hundred-plus-pound lion would be clearly visible, even at night. But as they got near the parking lot, he hunkered down and quickly crept across the lot, approaching the car from behind on the driver's side.

He could hear the three others heading back to the car now, complaining to the guy in the car about how much he sucked.

Coming up to the door, Sean shifted back, jumped into the seat, put the car in gear. Grabbing the steering wheel with his left hand, he grabbed the guy in the right seat just as he started to yell, "He's *here!*" and slammed his head into the dashboard a couple of times until he stopped moving.

As soon as he got off campus, he turned left, turned the lights back on, and slowed down so as not to attract any attention. When he got to McCarran, he went east, and after a few blocks he turned down a small side street. Putting the car in park, he turned it off, unfastened the other man's seatbelt, dragged him out of the car, and quickly stripped him of his shirt, which he tore up and used one sleeve to blindfold him with. The man's face was pretty bloody; Sean could only guess that he'd broken his nose.

The other sleeve he used to bind the man's hands behind him. Then he went through his pockets, relieving him of his wallet, his cell phone, and a key ring with some keys. He took off the two rings the man was wearing, as well as the strange looking necklace, then searched the car.

On the floor, where he must have dropped it when Sean slammed his face into the dashboard, was a rag with dried blood on it. Sniffing at it, Sean realized it was his blood. Probably from the van.

'Before you became us,' his lion pointed out.

"Good point," Sean murmured.

The glove box didn't have anything beyond the registration, which Sean grabbed. The back seats had some drink containers, but the trunk had a couple of road flares in it, which Sean also grabbed.

By now the man was starting to groan, so Sean walked over to him.

"Where is my mom?" Sean asked.

"What?" the man gasped, his voice sounding different now. Sean wondered if he'd broken more than just his nose.

"My mother. You killed my neighbor, and you kidnapped my mom, where is she?" Sean asked, and for good measure he hauled off and kicked the guy in the side.

"I don't know where your mother is!" the man gasped.

"Look, you tell me where she is, I let you live. You don't, you die," Sean growled and kicked him again, harder.

"I swear," the man coughed, "I swear to you I don't know! We didn't kill him! That wasn't us!"

"Oh? You're tracking me down, sending men after me, you have my blood from the van, and you want me to believe you're not involved?"

Sean kicked him again, and he was pretty sure he felt a rib break; the guy gasped in obvious pain.

"Please! Please, don't kill me; I'm just a tracking mage! I don't know what's going on, they don't tell me anything! All I know is they wanted us to get you before the Lithos did."

"The Lithos? Who the hell are they?"

"I, I think they're some gang in Lithuania, I don't know! I'm just a hired helper! They said they had to get you first, but we weren't to kill you! Just bring you in!"

"How'd you get my blood?"

"I told them I needed something physical of yours, so we snuck into the impound lot and I used a spell to gather up all of your blood." He was babbling now, Sean guessed he really believed Sean was going to kill him.

"How did you hide from my spell?" the guy asked him suddenly as Sean tried to decide what to do with him.

"Trade secret," Sean told him. "Do you know why they want me?"

"No, no I don't!"

Sean prodded the spot where the broken rib was, making the man gasp in pain.

"Want to reconsider that answer?" Sean asked. "I'm not a very patient man anymore Mr.," Sean opened the wallet and looked at the license inside, "Mr. Smith. Damn, is that your real name?"

"Yes, it's my real name," he gasped. "And I don't really know, but I overheard someone saying something about they didn't want you finishing your father's work, that it was too dangerous!"

Sean looked in the wallet. There was a fair bit of money there; he took half of it and memorized the man's name and address. Surprisingly, he lived in Sparks.

"Okay, Mr. Smith, here's the deal. You get to live today," Sean heard him exhale in relief. "I am relieving you of some of your cash as a fine for helping them. Do it again and, well, I'll kill you. Also, I know where you live now, so don't think I don't know how to find you.

"Oh, one other thing. Who the hell hired you?"

"I can't tell you that!" he protested.

"Oh please, don't make me into a liar by forcing me to kill you after all. I want a name."

"The Vestibulum! It was the Vestibulum!"

Sean pondered that, it sounded like Latin; he'd have to look it up when he got home.

"Swear you'll never track me again."

"I swear! I, Richard Smith, swear I will never track you, Sean Valens, again! Ever!"

"Good. This isn't your car, is it?" Sean asked as he lit the first flare and tossed it into the front seat.

"What? No! What's that sound?"

"I'm starting a fire. You might want to get to your feet and start walking away before the gas tank goes up," Sean said as he lit the second flare and tossed it in.

"Oh, here's your wallet," Sean said. Picking the guy up, he stuck his rings, necklace, and wallet in his pocket and pointed him to the south. "Better start walking."

Sean tossed the third flare in, and took off running before Mr. Smith could pull off his blindfold, putting the now merrily burning car between them.

Sticking the bills in his mouth, he shifted again and loped off, heading home, making only a slight detour to hide the money on the roof of a bank by an ATM. Last thing he wanted was Smith trying to find Sean via the cash he'd stolen. Let him think he'd deposited it.

"Where have you been?" Roxy asked, sitting up in bed with her tail curled around her, as he pulled himself in through the window.

"Having fun," Sean purred, then shifted back.

"Is that smoke I smell?"

"Yeah, have you ever heard of a gang called the Lithos from Lithuania?"

"That's not a very original name." Roxy chuckled and shifted back into human form as well.

Sean shrugged. "That's what the guy I caught told me."

"Guy you caught?" Roxy asked, eyes wide.

"Yup, was easy too." Sean grinned. Coming over and sitting next to her on the bed, he told her about his encounter with Mr. Smith and the others working for the Vestibulum.

"Vestibulum means 'Static' in Latin." Roxy sighed. "I better call my dad, he'll know."

"I think that can wait until morning, don't you?" Sean grinned as he leaned in closer and started nibbling on the side of her neck.

Roxy sighed and slipped her hand into his lap. She started stroking him, not at all surprised to find him already excited.

"Yeah, why ruin his sleep?" Roxy agreed and let Sean pull her back down onto the bed.

Sweet Tuesday Morning

Jolene sighed and looked at the door; it said 'Sawyer's Antiquities' in faded green letters across the light gray metal. Easy to miss if you weren't looking for it, but then the place was in the back of an industrial park, so if you didn't know it was here, the odds of stumbling across it were slim.

She didn't like dealing with Sawyer, but she made a point of stopping here every month because Sawyer kept an ear on the comings and goings of all things magical in Reno. Some of that was so he knew what opportunities there might be out there, but most of it was simple self-preservation. Sawyer dealt in rare and illicit items, most of which were stolen, and he was fencing.

Squaring her shoulders, she pushed the door open and stepped inside.

As shops went, it looked like most pawn shops. There were rows of glass cases to either side of the room, and well as a center platform that held larger items. There were no windows, but the lights kept it from being too dim.

"Hi, Jolene."

"Hello, Marx," she said to the brutish looking fat man sitting by the door. Jolene knew he only *looked* human; he wasn't, Sawyer wouldn't employ humans, ever. Marx was a wereboar, and while he looked fat, Jolene knew he could move very quickly when he wanted to.

"Well, if it isn't my favorite harlot, fresh off the sheets no doubt, to grace my humble establishment!"

"Well, you're in a good mood today, Sawyer," Jolene said, taking her time as she strutted down the aisle towards the chest-high counter in the back. She didn't notice anything different in the displays, but she wasn't surprised. They rarely changed, as their primary purpose was camouflage for what really went on here.

"Listen, Tart, I don't have time for you today. Can't you see I'm busy?" Sawyer waved his short arms around the empty store. Goblins weren't very tall. Sawyer stood all of four-foot, and for a goblin, he was a tall one. He was bald of course, most goblins were, and he almost looked normal in his expensive dress shirt and fancy silk tie. But his skin was green, and his nose and ears were both a little too long and a little too pointed to be human. With a large hat and the proper skin color, Sawyer would simply be a short, ugly human. But as goblins went, Jolene had heard he was considered to be rather handsome by the women of his race.

Not that she'd ever seen any here during any of her visits.

The floor behind the counter was set high, so Sawyer could loom over his clients, who were usually much taller than he was.

"I love you too, Sawyer." Jolene smiled at him. "So what has you in such a snit today? I thought you'd had a big score last week on some very juicy information?"

"And why would I tell a cheap floozy about that?"

Jolene laughed. "Oh please, they hate me just as much as they hate you; you know that. Besides, I might have some information on all the excitement that's been going on. Maybe we could work out a deal?"

Sawyer's eyes narrowed a bit. "And what would a tramp like you know?"

Jolene smiled and played with her hair a moment, then took a slow look around the store while ignoring his jibes.

"Well?" Sawyer demanded.

"Tramps like me, we get around Sawyer, you know that. You know those guys who died up in the schoolyard in Sparks?"

"Yeah, what about 'em?"

"They said that they were working for *you*."

Sawyer didn't give much away, but Jolene thought she could detect a slight hint of concern.

"They're all dead, who cares?"

"Well, the people who killed them, I'd think. So, Sawyer, why do you think they'd finger you in all of this?"

"Maybe I did a little business with them, what's it to you?"

"You doing business with humans? Sawyer," Jolene laughed, "are you slipping on me?"

"Money is money, it all spends the same. And it spends even better when I can get it by stirring up mischief with all those stuck-up mages!"

"Come on, Sawyer, no freebies. I got some hot info for you, but first you gotta tell me what you did."

"Just how hot are we talking?" Sawyer was all ears now.

"Hot enough to burn you." Jolene smiled.

"Okay, Okay," Sawyer said. "But this'd better be good, or you ain't ever walking in here again!

"Ya see, there used to be this big mage in town, high powered alchemy type. But the councils and all, they didn't like him much. Said he consorted with the 'animals' too much."

Jolene clearly heard Marx snort from over by the front door.

"So, word got out he was working on something the councils didn't like, and one of them had him rubbed out."

"They killed him?" Jolene exclaimed in shock.

"Well, they didn't kill him themselves; they're too prissy for that. They hired some guy from Chicago to come out here and deal with it for them."

Jolene nodded. "Okay, but that's all ancient history; what does that have to do with today?"

"Simple, they didn't kill his wife and kid. Oh, they did a number on them; put them in the poor house!" Sawyer laughed, "I bet that must have been quite a shock for a couple of humans, going from rich and pampered to being broken bums! But the kid, the kid's about to turn twenty-one, and a couple of those seer types on the magic councils and in the wizard gangs? They said that the kid is gonna find something from his old man's work, finish what he started. They either want to stop him or get their hands on it. Take your pick."

"And what's your part in this?"

"I told them how to find the kid, that's all. Wasn't hard either," Sawyer laughed, "I just looked them up on the internet! Took me all of five minutes, and I got a quarter-mil out of those idiots! Some geniuses! They can't even figure out how to use Google!

"Now give," Sawyer said.

"What was it his father was making?"

"Not another word until I heard what you got!" Sawyer growled.

Jolene smiled. "That kid? He's dating a friend of mine."

"Awesome! I can earn another couple hundred thou! I'll even split it with ya! What's the address?"

"Her name is Roxy Channing."

"Ya, okay, that helps, I can use Google if you don't want to rat her out."

Jolene laughed. "Sawyer, for a goblin that sells intelligence, you are one damn stupid idiot, do you know that?"

"He's a human, Jolene. There's no need to be getting sentimental on me. So he's dating some broad that you know? Call her up and take her out for lunch or something, I'll make sure she's left alone."

Jolene sighed and rolled her eyes. "She's Bill Channing's daughter. You know, your 'friend' down in Las Vegas? The *Sheriff?*"

Sawyer froze, and his eyes suddenly got very wide.

"Did you just say that this kid is dating Sheriff Channing's daughter?"

Jolene nodded.

"But, she's a lycan, like her dad! And this kid's a human! Lycans and humans don't date! They just don't!"

Jolene smiled at him. "Actually, it's more like 'mated' at this point. They've kinda moved on past the dating stage."

Jan Stryvant

"You telling me that the kid is a lycan?" Sawyer said, and Jolene could see he was starting to sweat.

"Yup."

"That ain't cool, Boss." Marx said from his seat at the other end of the store.

"Screw that!" Sawyer yelled. "We're talking about Tooth and Claw Channing! He threw me out of Vegas just 'cause I mentioned to that Paulson idiot that he had a daughter! If he finds out I'm involved in..."

Sawyer looked at Jolene. "Please, Jolene, Honey, tell me he doesn't know, that you're the only one!"

"Sorry, Sawyer. The guy who ratted you out before he died?"

"Uh oh," Sawyer said and swallowed.

"Yeah, Roxy killed him."

"Marx! Get up off your ass! Bar the door! We're going on a vacation! NOW!"

Jolene almost laughed as Sawyer started to gather up a bunch of things and throw them into a suitcase he'd pulled out from under the counter.

"Thanks for the info, Kid. I gotta run, the backdoor's through there!" Sawyer said, jerking his thumb over his shoulder.

"So, just what is this work that the kid is supposed to do?"

"I ain't got time for that now, I gotta run!"

Jolene laughed as Sawyer closed the suitcase, grabbed a hat, and stuck it on his head.

"Oh, right, laugh it up, rub some salt into the wounds why don't 'cha."

"Sawyer, did you hear me say she's a friend?"

"Ya, so?" Sawyer said heading for the back door. Marx was already there, and he had a much larger suitcase in hand.

"She's a *very* close friend, *very* close."

"What are you telling me?" Sawyer stopped and turned, eyeing her warily.

"I could talk to her, tell her you didn't know, get her to tell her father to back down and leave you alone, perhaps?"

"You'd do that for me? Why?" Sawyer asked, looking suspicious.

"'Cause you're probably the only person in town those sanctimonious bastards hate more than me." Jolene laughed.

"And that's the only reason?"

"Well, now that you mention it, there are a few questions you could answer."

"I don't know what they're afraid of; I don't know what his old man was working on. Whatever it is, it's something that they've been keeping secret for a long time now. It had something to do with the Lycans."

"What? Something bad?"

"Hardly! That guy loved lycans! Had several of them working for him, word was his best friend was a lion-were. No, something that was going to help get the human mages and wizards feet off their necks. Change the status quo."

"And you were helping them stop this, Boss?" Marx growled and looked down at Sawyer, who rolled his eyes.

"Look, I don't believe that the kid has squat or will do squat. I thought he was just another human kid doing human things. If they'd had something like that, they would have sold it off years ago. It's a myth, okay?"

"What if it's not a myth?" Marx growled.

Jolene held up her hand, interrupting the budding argument.

"Do you know who's after him?" Jolene asked Sawyer.

"Everybody. Every magic user's council, good and bad, their criminal gangs, all of them, or damn near all. They either want to get it for themselves to gain more power over the lycans, get it to stop it from ever getting out, or they just want to stop him. And a lot of the groups out there aren't picky over *how* they stop him, either. They killed his father, right? So why would they worry about killing his kid?"

"Boss," Marx started, but Sawyer did a sudden double-take and held up *his* hand.

"Wait a moment; you said this kid is a lycan now, right?"

Jolene nodded.

"And if they're worried about him, that means he's a magic user?"

Jolene shrugged. "It's a possibility, why?"

"A lycan magic user? Are you kidding?" Sawyer howled with laughter. "Oh man! Would that ever get their panties in a bunch!

"Tell you what, Jolene, if this kid does come up with something, bring him here and I'll make sure every damn lycan in the state gets whatever the hell it is."

"For a price, of course," Jolene said wryly.

"Hell yeah! Of course for a price! I'm not doing charity work here! But don't worry, Marx here will probably kill me if I try to rip anybody off."

Jolene looked at Marx, who nodded. "When it comes to family, I keep him reasonably honest."

Jolene nodded. "Okay then."

Sawyer smiled. "Sure, Hon, anything. Just as long as you get Sheriff Channing off my ass."

"You learn anything, you let me know, okay?"

Sawyer smiled, and actually looked happy. "Jolene, darling? You keep that crazed cheetah from killing me and it's a deal!"

Jolene smiled and stuck out her hand, which Sawyer quickly shook.

"Have a nice day, gentlemen!" Jolene smiled, turned, and started walking slowly back towards the front door as she pulled out her cell phone to call Roxy.

"Yes, Jolene?" Roxy answered.

"Could you do me a favor, Hon?"

"Sure, what?"

"Could you call your father and tell him to leave Sawyer alone?"

"And just why would I want to do that?"

"Because he's being more than helpful. In fact, you might even say he's on our side."

"Oh! I gotta go then!" and Roxy hung up.

Stopping at the barred door, Jolene looked back at Marx, who looked at Sawyer, who nodded at him.

Walking down to the front door, he unbarred it and opened it, then jumped back a good ten feet. There was a werecheetah in the doorway, a very large and well-armed one, with a cell phone to his ear.

"If that's what you want, Honey, fine, I won't bother him at all."

"Why, Sheriff Channing, so nice to see you again." Jolene smiled. "Could you give me a ride home, perhaps?"

Sawyer watched wide-eyed from the back of his shop, hiding behind the counter.

"Why, I'd be delighted to, Jolene."

Marx closed the door behind Jolene as she walked off with the Sheriff and turned to look at his boss, who was panting behind the counter and wiping his brow.

"Next time, Boss, maybe you should do more than just Google it?"

"Oh, shut up and watch the door."

Tuesday at School

Sean was on pins and needles all day at school; Tuesday was his heavy day, with the most classes. He was constantly on the lookout, to the point he was having a hard time following what his teachers were going over.

"Something the matter, Sean?" Professor Cruz asked him as he left his last class of the day.

Sean sighed. "My mother's house was robbed, and now she's missing, and her next-door neighbor, a close family friend, was found shot dead.

"Oh, and my girlfriend's father, who's a sheriff, thinks I should drop out and lie low until the police figure out what the hell is going on."

Sean looked at the shocked expression on his professor's face.

"You're not kidding, are you?" Professor Cruz asked.

Sean shook his head. "I wish I was."

"I think you should take his advice. You obviously feel like you're in danger."

"But there's only a few weeks in the semester until finals!"

"Five is not a 'few', Sean."

"One of those is Spring break," Sean pointed out.

"What are you taking this semester?"

Sean ran down the list; he had four computer science major courses, two social science electives, and a history course.

"Drop the history course and the social sciences. You can do those any time. All of us in the comp-sci department post our lecture notes after each class. You've been doing well enough, I'll let you take the final online. I'll talk to your other instructors. Do you have a detective I can call to verify your story?"

Sean dug out Detective Schumer's card and gave it to him. "Do you think they'll let me do it?"

"If you've been carrying a good average in class, I don't see why not."

Sean nodded and suddenly felt a lot better about things.

"Thanks, Professor. I appreciate the help."

"Eh, you're not the first student to come through here who was having problems like these. This may not be Vegas, but with all the gambling, Reno gets its own share of gang problems."

"Well, thanks anyway," Sean said. After checking his phone for messages, he left, heading home for the day.

He was attacked ten feet outside the building.

Sean was down on his knees before he'd even realized what was happening, having been hit in the back of the head with a club. The only reason he was even conscious was because of his new lycan stamina. He fell forward and tried to crawl away as people started yelling, when he suddenly felt paralyzed. Some sort of force was holding him still, not allowing him to move. He almost shifted, but there were people screaming, yelling, and running around, so the last thing he wanted to do was become *the* target in all of the confusion.

Which a huge lion would undoubtedly be.

Instead, he closed his eyes, let his body collapse to the ground, and started listening. He could hear people yelling to call an ambulance, and to 'catch that guy', so his best guess was that other students were getting involved.

"I'm a doctor! Let me through!" someone called, and Sean sighed. Hopefully by the time the police and an ambulance showed up, whatever this effect was that was paralyzing him would wear off.

He heard a siren then, surprised at how quickly they'd gotten there, but then, there had been an increased police presence on the school grounds again today, so they must have just had one in the area.

"Out of the way! Coming through!" someone was calling.

He felt them roll him onto his back, then a couple of people picked him up and put him on a stretcher.

"Hey, aren't you going to use a backboard?" someone in the crowd yelled.

"It's a head injury!" the doctor said, and Sean felt the straps across his body and his legs tighten down, and they were rolling.

He felt the jolt when they put him in the back of the ambulance and heard the doors close. A moment later he heard the front door close, the ambulance's engine started up, and the ambulance moved off.

"We clear?" the doctor asked.

"Yeah, we're clear. They bought it," said a second voice.

"Did our guy get away?"

"Scott? Yeah, he took off after he hit him. By the time anyone realized what was going on, he had a big head start."

"Now what?" asked a third voice.

"Now we take him back and let the experts take him apart. That's what," the second voice said.

"Can I drop the paralysis spell?" the doctor asked. "It's pretty tiring."

"Yeah, these straps are pretty tight; even if he comes to, he's not getting out of that!"

Sean felt the spell release him. Opening his eyes, he looked around; there were three of them, alright. None of them had guns out; only one appeared to have any kind of suspicious bulge.

"Ah, awake I see. You've been giving us a hard time, Mr. Valens; you've been giving us a *very* hard time."

Sean identified him as the second voice; he was the one with the gun. The 'doctor' was sitting by his head; the third person was sitting down by his feet. Sean was being held to the stretcher by two straps, which he guessed were locked in place. The three men were sitting on a bench seat on the other side of the vehicle from him, about two feet away. Probably where real paramedics would have sat.

And it was a real ambulance. He could see all the gear was in it, the oxygen regulators, everything. He wondered where they'd stolen it from.

"If you let me go now, I won't kill all of you." Sean said, embracing his lion. He had no doubt after hearing that 'take him apart' line that whatever they had planned for him, he wasn't going to like it.

"You're hardly in a position to talk!"

"Sure," Sean growled and started looking at his options. "So, are you with the Lithos, the Vestibul-whatever the hell, or are you a new player in this party?"

The man laughed. "I gather the Lithos have gone home to lick their wounds. Showing up at the mall was really a bad idea. We're with the council of Gradatim."

"More Latin, right?" Sean said and tested his bonds.

"Don't bother; you're not going anywhere, Mr. Valens."

"You know my father left me nothing, right? And we were stripped of everything we had?"

"That may be, but we'll still make sure. Don't worry, it'll be painless, I promise."

"I won't be," Sean growled. Embracing his lion, he let the rage he was feeling fill him as he shifted.

It felt different. He wasn't in the back seat this time, he was front and center, but so was his lion. There was no separation between the two of them, and it felt *right*. He sat up as the belt around his chest snapped, reached down with a large fur covered hand, and sliced the belt over his legs with a finger.

Rolling onto his left side, he kicked out his right leg with his claws out, and effortlessly disemboweled the one sitting at the back as he struck the man who had been talking with his right fist.

The man grunted, but apparently he was wearing body armor of some sort, because Sean's hand didn't go through his chest. Meanwhile, the 'doctor' at the head of the bench shrieked like a little girl and started beating on the partition door to the front.

The man he'd hit was fumbling with his gun as Sean growled and pulled himself closer to the man.

"Use your paralysis spell, you asshole!" the man yelled and started to chant something as well. Sean opened his mouth wide and roared in the man's face as he grabbed for the man's hand. Sean missed; his body was a lot bigger now, and he'd misjudged the grab, but they were nose to nose now. Opening his mouth, he took the man's head between his jaws, and bit down. Hard.

Hot blood and a foul taste filled his muzzle as the man's body jerked and the gun went off. Sean didn't feel any pain, so he'd obviously missed. Spitting out the crushed remains of the man's head, he turned and faced the 'doctor', who was gibbering in fear now.

"Don't kill me! Don't kill me! Don't kill me!"

"Where's my mother?" Sean growled.

"Don't kill me! Don't kill me! Please don't kill me!"

Lashing out, Sean punched him in the throat, crushing it. He'd been aiming for the mouth to shut the man up. He was definitely going to have to spend some time in this new form to get a better feeling for this new body.

The man fell to the floor, choking. Sean looked around for the gun; he figured the guy was as good as dead anyway. He found the gun in the other man's grip and quickly pried it out. It wasn't large enough for his new hand, but he couldn't stay like this much longer. He had to get out of the ambulance, and a huge lionman would be noticed.

Shifting back was a moment's thought, then he picked up the gun, turned, and looked at the partition door. Sliding forward, he opened it.

"What the hell are you doing to that kid back..." the driver said and turned to look at Sean, his eyes widening in surprise just as Sean shot him in the head.

The ambulance took off as the dying spasms of the man pushed the accelerator to the floor, then it started to rock side to side, throwing Sean, the dead bodies, and any gear that wasn't strapped down all over the back of the ambulance. After a few moments it must have hit something. There was a loud noise, it rolled over onto its side, and went sliding along the ground, everything inside falling to the left side of the ambulance as the sounds of scraping and tearing metal filled the vehicle.

Sean flew forward and hit the front bulkhead, when quite suddenly and with a very loud 'Bang!', the ambulance came to an abrupt stop. Hitting his head, he groaned in pain as several portable oxygen bottles slammed into him, breaking his arm and several ribs.

It took him a moment to gather his wits. There was a piece of metal trim sticking into his leg; grabbing that with his good arm, he pulled it out and looked around for an escape route. The side door was above him now; getting to his feet, he tried to avoid getting any blood on him as he reached up with his good arm, unlatched the door, and pushed it open.

That was when he heard it. A hissing noise. No, actually it was more like a whistling noise, like a bomb...

Reaching up with both hands, Sean grabbed the door and hauled himself out onto the top of the overturned ambulance. Amazingly, his arm seemed fine now. And the hole in his leg from the trim was gone. Even his head felt fine!

They were off the road a ways now, and suddenly he heard the sound of a fire igniting as the hissing noise got louder. He knew that oxygen didn't explode, but gasoline sure did, and if this thing was going to burn, he wanted to get as far away as he could. Jumping off the ambulance, he turned and ran away from the road, deeper into the brush and scrub, going just as fast as he could. He'd lost his shoes; they'd come off when he'd shifted. Surprisingly, his pants and shirt were fine. Other than being covered in blood and gore, of course.

But that could wait; the first thing was to get *away*. There were already people running down from the road to investigate, and some of them looked like they had fire extinguishers. The sounds of sirens were starting up in the distance.

Sean shook his head; sirens seemed to be the theme song of his life these days.

Eventually he figured out where he was and, remembering there was a lake in San Rafael Park, he started to run that way. By the time he'd gotten to it, just about everything had dried on him, but he didn't care. Right now he wanted it all *off*. Taking out his phone and setting it down with his wallet, he dove into the water.

It was so cold he nearly screamed. He was surprised he hadn't had a heart attack. Then again, maybe he had, and his lion had healed it? His lycan-ness had sure dealt with the other injuries he'd gotten quickly enough.

Surfacing, he treaded water as he worked all the dried blood and gunk out of his hair. Going under the surface a few times, he finally got it all out, when he realized he had another problem.

There were people waving and yelling at him from the far side of the lake, some of which were now coming around to where he was.

Sighing, he swam over to the side and pulled himself back up out of the water, wondering if they thought he was drowning or something? It's not like the water was deep, or even all that fresh! But it still beat the hell out of what he'd been drenched in before.

Picking up his phone and wallet, he left the park, heading back to the road. At least now he didn't look like a refugee from a slasher movie, he just looked like a wet, filthy, shoeless bum.

At least nobody looked at bums.

Looking at his phone, he saw several unanswered calls. He had his phone on silent mode while in class, it didn't even vibrate. He hadn't thought to turn the ringer back on until now though. The first one he called back was Roxy.

"Sean, are you okay?" were the first words out of her mouth.

"Well, I am now. Though I'm in desperate need of a shower and a change of clothes. Where are you?"

"I'm back at the apartment. Jolene is here too. We heard about what happened at the school."

"What's Jolene doing there?" Sean asked, his mood lifting. Hopefully she'd stay the night; he wanted to get his claws into her again tonight. As well as a few other things.

"She learned a few things, and you need to hear them."

"Okay, has anyone heard about the ambulance crash?"

"That was you?" Roxy said, surprised.

"Yeah, the attack was a setup to kidnap me using an ambulance. I suspect it was stolen."

"Yeah, it was stolen alright. They're saying meth-heads on the news right now."

"Well, that's good. I'll be there in about an hour. It's a long walk, and I'm tired."

"Okay, we'll be here."

"Order me a lot of food, please?"

"How much is a lot?"

"Oh, five or six meat pizzas will probably do it."

"Okay, Love. You take care."

Sean smiled; he really liked it when she called him love.

"You too, Love," he said and ended the call.

Next was Detective Schumer.

"Detective? This is Sean Valens."

"Ah, Sean! I just wanted to let you know we're done processing your mother's house, as well as Mr. Sampson's. You're free to go back there whenever you want.

Sean nodded to himself and sighed. He'd have to see about going by there and, at the very least, cleaning up the mess.

"Thanks, Detective."

"Oh, the casino had your mother's car towed back to the house. It still needs front tires, however."

"What about Sampson's car? They ever find that?" Sean asked.

"No. We've notified all the impound lots and scrap yards. It'll turn up eventually. We were contacted by his lawyer, however."

"He had a lawyer?" Sean was surprised to hear it.

"Yes, and he had a will. You're his sole beneficiary; I gave his lawyer your phone number, so you'll probably hear from him eventually. Anthony Barton is his name."

"Okay, I think I have a call from him to return, as well. Thanks detective. Any leads on my mom?"

"Sorry, Sean, we don't have any leads on that, but we found the gun that killed Mr. Sampson."

"Really? Where?"

"There was a van that crashed Friday night, you may have heard about it?"

"Yeah, I saw it in the paper."

"We recovered the gun from that wreck. One of the dead guys in it must have been the one that shot him. We still haven't figured out how their paths crossed, but I suspect once we find his car, we'll know."

"Okay, thanks Detective."

"Have a good day, Sean."

Sighing, Sean looked at the third call he'd had missed. Sure enough, it was the attorney.

"Anthony Barton, attorney at law," a man answered the phone.

"This is Sean Valens, you called me?"

"Ah yes, Mr. Valens. I was the late Mr. Sampson's attorney. As the state has notified me of his death, I'm in the process of executing his last will and testament."

"Okay, what does that have to do with me, Sir?"

"Well, simply put, you're his sole beneficiary."

Sean sighed. "I knew he didn't have any family. Other than the trailer he lived in next to ours, did he have anything else?"

"Not much, I'm afraid. His car, motorcycle, and whatever was in his house or on his property. I will need you to come by and sign some papers, but that's it."

"Okay, I'm a bit busy dealing with a few issues right now. Do you know what's going to be done with his body?"

"His last wishes were for it to be cremated and the ashes spread in the hills."

"Okay," Sean checked his surroundings; thankfully it was just cars going down the road. "Could you text me your address and business hours? I don't know when I'll be able to stop by, but I'll try to make it soon."

"Of course, Mr. Valens. And you have my condolences. I didn't know Mr. Sampson well, but he seemed to be a nice man."

"He was. Thanks." Sean sighed, closed his phone, and put it away. He turned down a side street, then cut across some of the fields. He wondered how long he had until the next attack.

"Oh man, do you stink!" Jolene said as he walked into his room. "What were you swimming in?"

"The lake in Rafael Park." Sean sighed and grabbed his towel. "I think we're gonna have to burn these clothes."

"Oh, I'm sure we can clean them up. It's just the crap from the pond there, right?"

"No, it's blood and guts. I jumped in the pond so I wouldn't look like a mass murderer and get arrested."

"How many?" Roxy asked.

"Four. These guys said they were from the Council of Gradatim; they also said that the Lithos had gone back home to lick their wounds."

"Well, go get cleaned up, we'll wait here."

Sean nodded, dragged his butt to the shower, and quickly washed himself off. Then, rolling his stinky clothes up, he wrapped the towel around his waist and ducked back into his room. Roxy took the clothes and ran down to the washroom in the basement with a bunch of soap and bleach to see if they could be saved, while he sat at his desk and started in on the first pizza with a will.

"So, what did you need to tell me?" he asked Jolene between bites.

"Well first of all, your father didn't die in an accident. He was murdered."

Sean stopped and turned to look at Jolene. "By who?"

"Some hitman from Chicago. But he was hired by one of the groups around here."

Sean growled at that. "What about all the other stuff that happened to us?"

"They set that up, too. They wanted to be sure you were never in any position to continue his work."

"And just what *was* his work?"

Jolene shrugged. "Sawyer didn't know, it was a big secret, but apparently it had something to do with lycans. You see, Sean, lycans are kind of on the low end of things in the supernatural world. They get a lot of raw deals and are treated pretty poorly by most magic users. Your father was trying to change that."

"And for that, they killed him?"

Jolene sighed. "You know how I get power from you?"

Sean smiled at her, remembering the other night. "I was sort of hoping to power you up some more tonight." He smiled.

"Yeah, well, there are other ways magic users can get power from lycans, and they aren't as nice or enjoyable. There are places where lycans live in complete thrall to wizards and mages. Your father was about to upset a very large apple cart. The criminal gangs that abuse lycans didn't want that; hell, a lot of the very prissy and stuck-up folks in the magical councils and communities here in this country don't want to see lycans in any situation where they can't take advantage of them at will."

Sean sighed. "And they think my dad left me whatever this thing is, and I'm gonna use it?"

"They all believe something is going to happen when you turn twenty-one, which will either leave you with the results of your father's work, or you're going to suddenly be able to finish it."

"Heh, like that's going to happen! They took everything from us, remember?"

"The other night, you regained something they took from you, Sean. What's to say you won't regain something else on your birthday? These people employ seers, people whose sole duty is to watch out for major events that'll affect their fortunes."

"And they say I'm going to do this thing?" Sean asked and thought about what she'd just said. His father had planned ahead; he was starting to see that now with the watch. Maybe his dad had employed a seer as well?

"Several of them have said this, yes," Jolene sighed, "and a lot of folks out there believe them. And they're acting on it."

"How many?"

"All of them."

Sean choked on his pizza. "How many is *all*?"

Jolene shrugged. "Hundreds? Thousands? Tens of thousands? I have no idea. There are about a dozen legitimate councils out there, legitimate in that they don't hide from the other councils or societies. They're big and have a lot of power. There are many more illegitimate councils that engage in dark or even evil practices, but no one knows how many because they tend to be small, often made up of only a handful.

"Then there are the gangs."

"Gangs?"

"As in all things human, you have organized crime gangs. The gangs tend to be made up of a mixture of magic users, normal humans who are wise to things or who have some minor gift, lycans, goblins, vampires, monsters, whatever."

Sean sighed and hung his head for a moment, until his stomach reminded him he was hungry, and he went back to eating.

'Gee, thanks dad,' was about all he could think of at that moment. It looked like he had

every magic user in the world after his scalp, and he was what? A twenty-year-old kid who'd never been outside of Reno, who had few friends and even fewer allies.

'You have me,' his lion reminded him, and Sean had to smile at that. He also had Roxy, and Jolene was helping. Then there was Roxy's dad. That would no doubt be worth quite a bit in the long run, as well.

Roxy rejoined them at that point. "Well, I don't think they'll be a total write off, but they're definitely going to have some stains. Bile is pretty nasty stuff."

"How do you get bile on your clothes?" Jolene asked, looking at the two of them.

"Don't ask," Sean and Roxy said at the same time, causing her to come over and hug him from behind as he started in on the second pizza.

"Did you tell him about the Council of Vestibulum yet?" Roxy asked Jolene.

"No, I thought I'd leave that to you."

"Oh," Sean interrupted, "today's attackers apparently came from the 'Council of Gradatim', whatever the hell that is."

Jolene sighed. "Oh great, the progressives have gotten involved."

"Progressives?" Sean asked.

"They like to call themselves that, but they're not really, they lifted it from some old political group to sound less offensive than they really are. They believe everyone should give their all to support their vision of the future."

"And what vision is that?"

"One where they rule like kings while the rest of us devote our lives to letting them maintain that lifestyle. All in the name of 'progress', of course."

"Of course," Roxy agreed. "Have you dealt with them before?"

"More than once. Usually, they're all talk and not much else. But when they get whipped up over something, well, ethics and morality go right out the window, not that they really have any. They can be pretty cruel. No doubt they see this as a chance to weaponize their lycans."

"Weaponize?" Sean asked, looking from Jolene to Roxy.

Roxy nodded. "You have to understand, Love, that there are lycans under the control of many of the councils. Some because they agree with the leaders, some because of the power they get from it, and many because they have no choice. The council leaders who want this 'thing', well, they may be thinking that if only they have it and the others don't, it will give their lycans an advantage over the others, which will allow them to rule over the other councils."

"Let me guess," Sean said, "lycans are the foot soldiers and cannon fodder who do all the fighting, while the mages all sit at home safe and secure?"

"That's the way of it." Roxy nodded.

"Then why am I, I mean *we*, running into mages out there instead of lycans?"

"Because if you really do hold the key to lycan freedom, the last thing they want is for any lycan to have control over it. The mages undoubtedly feel the temptation for a lycan to go rogue is too great to risk."

"Yeah, and who would blame them? So what's the story on the Vestibulum?"

"They're the largest of the councils, and the most powerful. They have smaller sub-councils in many cities, even here in Reno. They're very conservative in that they don't like change. They always seek to maintain the status quo."

"Well, at least they weren't shooting at me." Sean shrugged and picked up another slice of pizza.

"Yet," Jolene said.

Roxy nodded. "What Jolene said. They'll *usually* try to seek solutions that don't require violence, but only because they see violence as being too disruptive; it can stir up too much change for them. But they won't hesitate to kill to further their own ends, either. While they're slower to come to that decision, once they've made it, they tend to be all in."

Sean stopped and sat back for a moment, looking down at the second empty pizza box; he'd all but inhaled that one, as well. At least now he didn't feel like he was going to pass out at any moment.

Turning to face the girls he smiled. "As I see it, I have three major concerns right now."

"And those are?" Roxy asked.

"One," Sean pointed at Roxy, "two," he pointed at Jolene, "and three, staying alive so I can enjoy one and two!"

"Did you come up with that all by yourself?" Roxy asked, grinning.

"Right now, it's about all I can think of," Sean said, standing up and stretching as the towel that had been wrapped around his waist fell to the floor. "But I'm sure I'll have other ideas before the night is through," he said, leering at the two of them.

"You know," Jolene said, smiling as she started to undo her top, "I kind of like this idea. Roxy?"

"Oh, I think I'm gonna be liking it too!"

"Then maybe you'll like this even better?" Sean smiled and shifted; reaching out to his lion, they melded once more as he shifted into his hybrid form.

Jolene gasped and just stared at him.

The look in Roxy's eyes as she quickly stood up, shed her pants, and shifted into her hybrid form was one of pure lust.

"When did this happen, Sean?" Roxy purred as she got up. Pulling off her blouse, she started to run her hands over his strong, short-furred chest. "I really like the mane!" Roxy laughed, and grabbing it, she pulled his head down so they could kiss.

Sean rumbled happily. "While dealing with those bastards in the ambulance."

It took him a minute to figure out just *how* to kiss her; if people thought noses were bad, having a muzzle now made it a lot more difficult. You had to tip your head to the side a lot more.

On a more positive note, Sean realized as he finally achieved lip-lock – or perhaps it was now muzzle-lock – with Roxy, was that muzzles opened just a bit differently than mouths did and he had a much longer tongue now, as well. The tongue duel they engaged in as he wrapped his thicker and stronger furry arms around her, pulling Roxy tightly against him, was amazing.

Jolene watched in admiration. She'd seen Roxy's hybrid form before, of course, more than once and rather closely, to be honest. Roxy stood six foot as a cheetah-were hybrid, but Sean had to be over seven feet tall! Jolene was having trouble gauging it because of the way his lion's mane fluffed out around his head, and the way the two of them were now going at it.

Jolene watched as Roxy literally climbed up his body. Sean cupped Roxy's ass with one strong hand while the other twined in her blond hair, tipping her head back as he started to lick and nibble at her neck.

Sean just rumbled happily as Roxy grabbed at his shoulders and effortlessly lifted herself off the ground, wrapping her strong, sexy legs around his hips. Moving his attentions down to nibble at her neck had a definite effect on her, causing her hips to start grinding against his pelvis, and of course, his erection, which was trapped between them.

Spreading his legs a little wider for balance, he raised her up with the hand he'd cupped under her butt; she seemed to weigh almost nothing now. Roxy cooperated by loosening her legs a moment, reaching down, and guiding him into her heat. Roxy was more than ready for him, and as he lowered her, she wrapped her legs tightly around him once more. They made love standing there in the center of his room.

Jolene watched, her own arousal increasing, as Roxy and Sean loved each other, both of their tails lashing in excitement. It was one of the most erotic things she'd ever seen in her life, the large lion planted almost like a tree before her, his body thick with heavy muscles, and the sexy svelte cheetah wrapped around him moving up and down, grinding her body back down against his.

Just one very large, and very sexy, statue.

Up until this moment, Jolene hadn't realized just how deeply Roxy felt for Sean. Oh, she knew Roxy liked him, enjoyed his company as well as having him in her bed, and Sean of course was obviously and blatantly besotted with Roxy. But the way they held one another, the words of love that were being gasped, well, it might have only been a few days, but Jolene realized Roxy hadn't been joking when she'd told Jolene that Sean was hers now, and that Roxy was his.

Which meant, Jolene realized with a sudden and even larger shock, that those hints of *her*, Jolene, ending up as Sean's as well, hadn't been jokes. She'd heard lycans could form pair bonds, actually mating, very quickly, and now she'd seen it with her own eyes. She knew for certain that Sean wanted her as he wanted Roxy, and now she suddenly realized just what he wanted her for.

And all Jolene could do was sit and watch the two of them, her own lust rising, unsure whether she should run or stay and submit to what might now be inevitable.

There was no doubt Sean was a handsome man, as well as a handsome lycan. Jolene already had strong feelings for Roxy; with all the sex they'd had, it was hard not to. Jolene was sure Sean would *not* be willing to share her with other males, but then again, with the amount of power she got from Sean, and from Roxy, did she really need anyone else in her life anymore? Her master had told her, the night he'd let her go after her training was complete, that while physical love was a powerful thing for a tantric sex practitioner, should she ever find a deep, spiritual love with another, it would overshadow all that had come before.

When Roxy and Sean finally shivered and shook, calling out their love for one another, they both stood there a moment, panting and catching their breath.

Setting Roxy down carefully on the bed as she unwrapped herself from him, Sean looked over at Jolene, who was sitting there, wide-eyed, naked, and panting heavily, as if she'd just had an orgasm herself.

"Your turn," Sean purred.

Jolene nodded slowly. "Oh, yes, *definitely*," she panted, "but shift back first, you're so big you'll crush me!"

"I'll be gentle, never fear," Sean said, shifting back and carefully climbing onto the bed with the two of them.

Tuesday Night

They were sitting around on Sean's bed as they finished off the last of the pizza.

Sean felt oddly at ease for perhaps the first time since everything in his life had been turned upside down. Had it really only been four days ago? There were people after him, apparently a lot of people, he'd realized, while lying in bed with Roxy and Jolene after making love to both of his women.

Even that realization, that they were both his, didn't bother him. Perhaps this was a sign of what it meant to be, to be *integrated* with his new aspect? His lion? Or was it just the side effect of having spent a couple of wonderful hours making love and having sex with two absolutely beautiful women?

Jolene had just finished relating to him everything that had happened at Sawyer's earlier that day. Her comments about Marx's reactions, while made more as a joke about Sawyer's ability to get himself in trouble at times, made Sean realize he did have allies in what was coming.

He also realized he needed to delete his Facebook page and all the rest of his social media accounts. There might be a time for that stuff later, but that time wasn't now.

"So, now what?" Roxy asked, rubbing her leg against his foot.

"Well," Sean sighed, "I think I'm going to be dropping out of college."

"Really?" Roxy exclaimed. "But I thought you'd said no?"

Sean shook his head. "After today, I can't set foot on campus anymore. One of my profs offered to help me do my core courses by internet, and I may take him up on that, if I can. But until this is done, I'm finished there."

"I'm sorry, Love," Roxy said, leaning forward and putting her hand on his knee.

"I'm sorry too, Sean," Jolene said and rubbed his other knee.

"Well, to be honest," Sean said, smiling as he patted both of their hands. It was kind of hard to feel sorry for one's self while sitting cross-legged on a bed with two beautiful naked women. "I need to start studying the books my father left me. If this fight's going to involve magic, I need to start learning about it. That just isn't going to leave me with a lot of time for college."

"Dad did say that alchemists make a lot of money..." Roxy smiled, trying to encourage him.

"Especially as there's only one in town these days," Jolene agreed.

Sean nodded. "Well, even if it wasn't, until we can figure out some way to solve this whole thing, I can't go to school. It's not just that I'm a target there, but how long until other people get hurt? We saw what happened at the mall. If these people get desperate..."

"And they will," Jolene interrupted with a heavy sigh.

"I'd be endangering a lot of innocent people."

"But just how do we end it?" Roxy asked. "It's not going to end when you turn twenty-one, Sean. It's not going to end until they either own you or stop you."

"Oh, I can think of one way to stop them." Sean smiled.

"And that would be?"

"Jolene already told us that Sawyer would be more than happy to sell whatever we come up with; we give it to him and let him do just that."

"I'm not so sure Sawyer would survive that," Jolene pointed out.

"Okay, we put it up on the internet, share it with the world. You've already told us most of the people in the magical communities don't use it."

"You may have a point there." Jolene nodded.

"But what if it's not complete?" Roxy asked. "Then what?"

Sean shrugged. "We publish his notes? All of his work? Once I'm no longer the only person that has it, going after me becomes pointless."

"Or we just tell them that your father didn't leave you anything," Jolene said, "after your birthday passes. When is it, anyway?

"The twenty-third."

"The twenty-third? That's next week!"

"Yup," Sean nodded, "Friday. But no matter what I say, they're not going to believe any of it without proof. And the only way I can prove it is by succeeding. Until I do, they'll either think I'm still working on it, or I've succeeded and I'm sitting on it until the perfect time to strike."

"So we're stuck between a rock and a hard place then?" Roxy asked.

Sean smiled. "Maybe, but I can't think of anyone I'd rather be stuck there with than you two."

"But that still brings us back to 'what do we do next?'" Jolene asked.

"I like that you keep saying 'we'." Sean smiled and, leaning all the way forward, he put his hands to either side of hers and gave her a kiss as she blushed, before sitting back down.

"I think what we need to do is find someplace safer to live." Sean looked at them. "Spring break starts Saturday, and the school will turn into a ghost town. Even with Jolene's spell protecting this place, we'll still stand out like a sore thumb.

"And if they send some folks around looking for us, they'll find you pretty easily," Roxy agreed, nodding.

"So the question is, where do we go?" Sean looked at both of them as they stopped and considered it.

"Leave town?" Roxy suggested.

"And go where?"

"Las Vegas? My dad has quite a bit of power and connections there."

"And then I'm firmly associated with not only you, but with him and the rest of your family? I don't know if that's a good idea. Plus, Vegas is a pretty visible town; I'd rather stay out of sight. Besides which, if my father did leave me something, I'd think it's probably somewhere here in Reno."

"So what then? Go up into the mountains? Head up to the Tahoe forest?"

"Well that would certainly drop us out of sight!" Sean laughed.

"Yeah, but we'd be easier to find," Jolene said.

"But we wouldn't have to worry about witnesses, so we could deal with them firmly," Sean growled, grinning evilly.

"Down boy!" Jolene laughed. "You haven't been a lycan a week yet. You've got a lot to learn about fighting, I'm sure. Besides, while *you two* might be more than fine with going au naturel and living in the woods. I'm more of a city girl, without the benefit of a natural fur coat."

"I could change that for you," Sean said, still grinning.

"Sean! Really!" Jolene gasped, just a little surprised. The idea that he'd want to infect her, change her, had never once entered her mind!

"Well, sooner or later," he said with a wink, "I'd think you'd want to join the 'wild side.'"

Roxy snorted and smiled, then patted both Sean and a slightly shocked Jolene on the knee. "I think that's a conversation for another time, Okay? So, Jolene, do you have an idea?"

Jolene shook herself and looked at Roxy. "Yeah, we stay in town. With all of the people here, it makes us harder to find, Sean and I are both locals, and you've lived here more than long enough to know how to find your way around. I'd say we either find something in one of the business districts, because it's cheap with lots of inside space to defend ourselves, or maybe in or near one of the casinos, because it's crowded with lots of security."

"And lots of cameras." Sean sighed. "I don't think any of us want me or Roxy showing up on camera in the fur."

"Hmm, good point; I hadn't considered that. Okay, one of the business districts."

Sean nodded. "Well, that's a start. Anything else?"

Roxy nodded. "Yup. Range time."

"Range time?" Jolene asked, confused.

"Pistol range."

"Oh!"

"We need a car," Roxy grumbled. They'd gotten their holsters on, guns loaded, and found out that the nearest pistol range was about two miles away.

Sean was about to agree, then remembered. "We have a car."

"We do?" Roxy asked as he got out his phone.

"Yeah, my mom's car. But it's got two flats; hold on a moment."

Opening his phone, he dialed Steve.

"Sean!" Steve said, answering the phone. "Where have you been hiding yourself? We missed you Friday night!"

"Didn't Alex tell you?"

"Tell me what? I haven't talked to anybody since Friday. Terri and I spent the weekend with her parents, and I was slammed yesterday with work here at the garage. A couple of our regular customers got their windows broken in that big dustup at the mall over the weekend, so I had my guys working on them, along with all the typical morning stuff."

Sean nodded to himself; Steve had gone to work for his father right out of high school and had taken over the auto repair business his dad had spent years building up. Steve had done so well that his father had just left his son to it, bought a sailboat, and now Steve's parents were sailing around the world. Last he heard, they were in New Guinea.

"First off, my mom's car is at home with two slashed tires, happened at work and they had it towed back to the house yesterday."

"And they didn't repair 'em for ya?"

"Not from what the detective told me." Sean sighed.

"Detective!" Steve exclaimed loudly. "What the hell happened, Sean?"

"Mom's missing, Sampson's dead; someone shot him to death up in Sparks."

"What!"

"Also, the house was broken into, ransacked. So was Sampson's, but he caught the guys in the act. The police found *their* dead bodies inside."

"You're shitting me! Sampson's dead? I can't believe it! Do they think this has something to do with your mom missing?"

"Yeah, it probably does." Sean sighed.

"Dude, if there is *anything* I can do for you, *anything*, just say the word man, and it's done. I'll send one of my guys over there to replace the tires right now, free. It's on me man, don't worry about it. Are you holding up okay? Do you need a place to stay? You can always crash at my place; Terri likes you, she won't mind."

"Thanks, Steve." Sean smiled to himself. Steve was his oldest friend, a lot of kids had looked down on him too, because Steve's dad was a 'simple mechanic'. When Steve's dad gave Steve a Ferrari as a graduation present, a lot of kids suddenly discovered just how much a 'simple mechanic' who owns one of the largest shops in Reno actually makes. Several of their former classmates were now on Steve's payroll.

"But I'm staying with my girlfriend right now."

"Girlfriend? Oh yeah, that's right! Man, what didn't happen to you this weekend?"

"Yeah, I know. Up until I got a call from the police on Sunday, life was going good," Sean sighed. "Honestly, she's been a lifesaver."

"Well, any woman who'll stand by you through this is without a doubt a lifesaver. Better get a ring on her finger quick, man!"

"Oh, I will. Trust me on that one, Steve! Look, I need to run; I got a million things to do here."

"Gotcha! Just remember, if you need it, call. Anytime, day or night, ya hear?"

"Thanks, Steve."

"Hey, that's what friends are for, bud. Later!"

"Well, that takes care of that." Sean sighed and put the phone away.

"Is he serious about helping you?" Roxy asked.

"Yeah, Steve and I go way back. With my going to college and him taking over his dad's business, we don't see each other as much as we used to. But I've had to go out more than once in the middle of the night when I was in high school to help him out of a jam."

"Well, that's nice and all, but it still doesn't help us get where we're going."

"I guess the only thing we can do is walk and flag down a cab if we see one?" Sean said as Roxy grabbed her jacket and nodded.

"We need to get you a hat," she said, looking up him, thinking, "and maybe some glasses or something. It'll make you less obvious."

"Uh huh. Hey, does Jolene have a car?"

Roxy stopped and looked at him. "You know, I have no idea. So, off to the indoor range, get some practice in, then to get your mom's car?"

"Yeah, and if possible, I'd like to get Jolene to do to my mom's house what she did to our apartment building."

"*And* the car," Roxy added.

"Ewww, have sex in my mom's car?" Sean said, making a face.

Roxy shoved him. "You are such a goof. Now, keep your eyes open, and hopefully we won't have any fights today."

Home - Again

It was after lunchtime when they finally got to Sean's mother's house. Roxy paid the driver as he got out and looked at the car. It didn't have two new tires on it, it had four. Sean shook his head, but he wasn't surprised; knowing his mom, the back tires had probably been almost bald.

There was some sort of yellow device over the doorknob to Sampson's house with the words 'Police' on it, and a sign on the door saying 'Crime Scene, Do Not Enter.'

Getting out his keys and going up the steps to his mom's front door, he unlocked the door. With Roxy following him, he stepped inside.

The place was still a mess, but less of a mess, if that was possible. Before, everything had just been tossed all over the place; now at least it was stacked and ordered in piles all against the back wall.

"Well, it was nice of them to organize things at least." Sean sighed.

"Makes it easier for them to tell what they've gone through, or haven't," Roxy said.

"Let's check the kitchen; if there's any food, I'm hungry. Lock the door."

"I don't think that door will stop anybody, Sean."

"Yeah, but we'll hear them kicking it in."

Roxy tipped her head to the side in a shrug. "Good point."

The mess in the kitchen was less. Apparently one of the detectives had an OCD streak, as the dishwasher had been loaded and run. Opening the refrigerator, there was food, and it all looked fine.

"Might as well cook all this meat before it goes bad," Sean said. Pulling out the skillet, he turned the electric burner on, and tossed a ham steak in, leaving a second one on the counter for when it was finished. Raiding a few more things, he set them on the table.

"Well, let's see the rest of the mess," Sean said, leaving the food to cook as he went through the rest of the trailer.

Surprisingly, both his old bed and his mom's bed had been made. All the dirty linens had been folded and put in a pile on the floor. There wasn't much in his old room, he hadn't had much to start with, and most of what he had was now in his apartment.

His mother's room, however, would take quite a while to clean up, and Sean really didn't see the point, either she'd come home and fix it herself...

Or she was dead, and it would all just go into the trash.

It hit him then; why it had taken so long, he didn't know, but suddenly he realized that his mom was missing, probably dead. Sampson *was* dead, he'd seen his body.

Suddenly he couldn't see anything, it was all too blurry, and he was starting to gasp and choke.

"Sean, are you okay?" Roxy said, coming over to him.

"No, no I'm not," he said, trying not to lose it completely. "They're dead. They're all *dead!* Everyone is gone. It wasn't enough for them to kill my father, take everything we owned, destroy us completely, no, they had to come back and kill the only family I had left!"

Sobbing then, he buried his face in Roxy's chest and held onto her as he cried. His old life was gone; nothing would ever be the same. All he'd wanted to do was get a decent job, find a cute girl, and settle down. He didn't want to be famous; he didn't want to be anybody different from anybody else.

He didn't want to have to worry about whether there'd be food on the table each morning, or if there'd be a roof over his head each night.

And they took that from him, they took it all. Along with his father, Sampson, and his mother. They took his mother! Probably one of the most harmless people in the world, who'd endured years of suffering, and never once complained.

"I'm going to kill them," Sean gasped, "I'm going to find them, and I'm going to kill them *all.* I don't care who they are, where they are, I'm going to find them and I'm going to tear their fucking heads off, Roxy.

"I'm going to make them fucking pay. For what they've done to me, my family, and what they're trying to do to us now."

"Don't worry, Sean," she whispered and patted his head; "I'll hold them down for you."

Sean gulped and caught his breath, then looked up at her and smiled. "You will, won't you?"

Roxy smiled with a fierce expression he hadn't seen since she'd plotted to lure the men hunting them into a trap.

"I love you, Sean. You're my mate, my man. Anyone who fucks with you deserves to die. That's just the way it is."

Sean nodded and kissed her, then gave her a tight hug.

"We better flip that steak, or it might catch on fire," she warned him.

He nodded and let her go, then got up and went into the bathroom and washed his face.

"I'm sorry," he said and gave her a hug.

"Don't be," Roxy said, "I was starting to wonder if you had any feelings left, if you were capable of grieving anymore."

"It's just been so unreal, all of this."

"Even me?" she teased, leading him back to the kitchen.

"You've been the only shining light, the only real joy in this nightmare." he sighed, looking down at that cute butt of hers he'd admired for so long from afar.

"Oh? Forgot about Jolene already?" Roxy laughed. Coming into the kitchen, she picked up the skillet and, with a practiced toss, flipped the ham steak onto its other side.

"You'll always be number one, Roxy," Sean purred. Coming up from behind her, he put his arms around her. "I know there'll be others; my lion definitely wants to add Jolene, and well…"

"You want her too!" Roxy laughed.

"Yeah." He smiled and kissed her on the side of the neck, letting his hands cup her soft breasts.

"It's okay, Love. I knew when I first scoped you out that lions are like that."

"And still you brought me home?" Sean was a little surprised by that, but then he was still surprised he had Roxy. And he did have her; both he and his lion knew it.

"Sean, I grew up with a very dominant, and at times overbearing, father. You were attractive before this happened; I always thought you were cute, but you were always acting like you were trying to hide something, and nothing makes a girl curious like a secret. But you were human, and well, cross-dating rarely works out.

"But when you became a lion?" Roxy leaned back against him. "I like strong men, and I like dominant men. You're the first man my father hasn't run off. I knew he wouldn't be able to, hell the moment he met you, *he* even knew he wouldn't be able to, I could see it in his eyes.

"Besides, lions aren't the only ones who have multiple wives; my granddad had two. Probably why my father isn't as upset as some other lycan fathers might be."

Sean nibbled some more along Roxy's neck, causing her to sigh and lean back further into him.

"Why don't you put that on the side and we can go…" Sean started, thinking maybe he could finally 'christen' his old bed, when someone knocked on the door.

Sean growled and was surprised at how fast the gun appeared in Roxy's hand.

"Enemies don't knock." He sighed.

"The dangerous ones do," Roxy countered.

"Louise? Are you home?" A woman's voice came through the door.

"Mrs. Brently." Sean said.

"Gossip?"

"And then some, but she bakes cakes and cookies and loves to share." Sean smiled and, after giving Roxy a kiss on the head, he went over to the door and opened it.

"Sean! I thought I saw you! Is your mother home?"

"Hello, Mrs. Brently. No, my mom isn't home. I don't know if the police told you, but my mom's a missing person right now."

"Oh, dear!" Mrs. Brently said, holding her hand up to her mouth. "Everyone heard about what happened to poor Gregory, we'd been hoping your mother was just staying with you until the police had cleaned everything up."

"I'm sorry, but no."

"How are you holding up, Sean? Is everything okay?"

"About as okay as it can be, I guess."

"Sean, dinner's ready!" Roxy called from the kitchen.

Mrs. Brently blinked. "Who's that?"

"Oh, that's my fiancée."

"Fiancée? I had no idea, Sean. Well, congratulations!"

Sean smiled. "Thank you. I'd invite you in, Mrs. Brently, but I still haven't cleaned up the mess from the detectives, and well, I'm still dealing with everything that's been going on."

"That's okay, Sean. I'll let you go eat. My prayers are with you and your mom."

"Thanks," Sean said and closed the door. Locking it, he headed back to the kitchen.

"Thanks for the save." Sean sighed. Taking the plate Roxy handed him, he kissed her, sat down and proceeded to eat while she cooked the other ham steak for herself.

"We really can't stay here long." Sean said after they'd finished eating.

"No, we can't," Roxy agreed. "Is there anything you need? Anything you want to get?"

Sean sighed and shook his head. "When you grow up with nothing, it's kind of hard to make attachments to things." He took a moment to look around. "Well, let's clean up and get out of here. We can hit the lawyer's office, then get back to the apartment."

"Lawyer?"

"Sampson had a will, and apparently I'm the sole heir."

"I thought he didn't have anything to leave anyone?"

"Well, I think he owned the trailer, he had a car and a motorcycle as well. Beyond the books and clothing in his house? I don't think he had all that much. But if he left it to me," Sean shrugged, "I might as well get it. Not like I've got a lot anyway."

Sean grinned. "And we can't keep robbing the corpses of our enemies; sooner or later we'll run out of them!"

Roxy laughed, getting up to help him rinse the dishes and put them in the dishwasher. Then Sean grabbed one of the extra sets of keys for the car. Locking up, they got in and drove off.

It didn't take them long to get to the lawyer's office, and thankfully he was in. The office wasn't terribly large or very fancy. There was a secretary, a small waiting room, and the lawyer's office. It was on the second floor of a nondescript office building with insurance agents' offices and other such stuff throughout.

"Ah, Mr. Valens," Anthony Barton, the attorney, said, standing up.

"Call me Sean, please, and this is Roxy," Sean said, shaking hands.

"Please, sit, Sean, Roxy," Barton said, sitting down himself. "Give me a moment to find the file, ah, here it is."

Barton pulled a folder out of his desk and laid it on the table. "It's all fairly simple, everything that was Mr. Sampson's is now yours; his home, everything in it, Car, Motorcycle, his tools for work, his bank account." Barton looked up. "I can have that transferred to your account if you wish."

Sean nodded, and looked at the piece of paper that Barton had pushed across his desk towards him.

"Just sign there and I'll see to the title transfers. Do you have a current address?"

"Just send it to my mom's house," Sean said, reading over the document; It *was* fairly simple and all rather cut and dried. "Just add two to Sampson's address, we lived next door."

Barton nodded. "Sure, not a problem."

Picking up a pen, Sean signed it and slid the paper back towards Barton.

"Oh, and here are the keys to Sampson's house, his car, motorcycle, and tool shed." Barton said, picking up an envelope and handing it to Sean.

"Thanks. Is there anything else?"

"Um, no, that would be it."

"Thanks," Sean said. Standing and sticking out his hand, he shook hands with Barton as he stood up.

"I hate to rush off like this, but well, the people who killed Sampson are trying to kill me, and until I know who the hell they are, there isn't a lot I can do about it."

"Are you sure about that?" Barton asked, looking at Sean. "The police seem to think he just stumbled on some tweakers robbing houses, killed the two in his house, went after the others, and they killed him for it."

Sean opened his mouth, about to say something, then remembered something he'd seen on a Netflix show. Pulling out his wallet, he took out a five-dollar bill and stuffed it in Barton's pocket.

"There, you're my lawyer now," Sean said and noticed that Barton suddenly looked a lot more serious.

"You're not making meth out in the desert, are you?"

"No, but I was there when Sampson was killed; he was saving me from being kidnapped. Apparently my father was actually murdered because of something he did, or was doing, and now they're suddenly afraid I'm going to do the same damn thing."

"If that's true, why don't you go to the police?"

"Because the police wouldn't believe me, just like you don't. Even if they did, they can't protect me; these are powerful people with lots of money."

"So what are you going to do?"

"What they're all afraid I'm going to do of course," Sean said, leaving the office, "what other choice do I have?"

Wednesday Afternoon

"Hon," Sean said looking over at Roxy, who was studying. "Take a look at this, would ya?"

"Sure, what is it?" Roxy said looking up.

"It's the fourth key from the envelope the lawyer gave me."

"The one for your friend's tool shed?"

"Sampson didn't have a tool shed; he didn't even have a garage." Sean sighed.

"Do you think," Roxy asked, picking up the key and looking at it, "that this is what everyone is looking for?"

Sean shrugged. "Maybe? I don't know. But if it is, how did Sampson manage to take it without everyone knowing about it?" Sean stopped and looked at the key in Roxy's hand. "I suspect it probably isn't, but it's obviously important."

"Well, maybe Jolene can help us out when she gets back."

"Yeah, I guess we'll just have to wait and see."

"Why don't you try studying for a while? Maybe it'll help."

"Eh, I'm probably dropping out; I don't see what the point is at the moment."

"I wasn't talking about school, Hon, I was thinking about those spell books you have. I'm surprised you haven't been diving into them every spare moment!"

Sean looked back at her sheepishly. When the spell had triggered last night, he'd immediately canceled it and gone back to sleep; he was just too tired after everything that had happened, not to mention what he'd done with the girls.

"Can you believe I keep forgetting to do it?"

"Well, I'm reminding you now!" Roxy said and pointed at him. "Study!"

"Yes, Ma'am!"

Laying back on the bed, Sean started thinking about the magical classroom his father had created.

Nothing happened.

Next he cast the spell he'd learned, and the magical spreadsheet, or what he was now thinking of as his stats sheet, opened. A quick look at that showed nothing had changed.

Closing that spell, he wondered a moment, could he only do this when he was asleep? If so, that would suck. Then he remembered that it all focused on the watch Sampson had given him, which his father had prepared. Raising his hand, he looked at the watch, and concentrated on the magical classroom.

It worked, and suddenly he was there once more. Looking down at his desk, there were now several books with names on each of them. Picking up the 'book' from the previous night, 'Mastery of Self', he skimmed it quickly; nothing new had appeared in it, so he set it back down.

Next he picked up one labeled 'An Introduction to Magic' and started to read that one.

As books went, it was fascinating to Sean. It talked about the structure of magic, starting first with where the power came from. Primarily it came from one's self, and some people, as well as some creatures, had more than others. It wasn't quite the power of life, because certain objects could be embodied with magical spells by alchemists, and the secrets of how they did so were closely guarded ones taught only from father to son.

Sean was a bit surprised to see that, for something that had apparently been around for thousands of years, no one really knew where the power came from. But then again, no one knew where gravity came from, but everybody inherently understood how it worked.

But that was just the introduction; the next part talked about spells.

Spells were all about using a language, which had a structure, a syntax, and a series of simple commands that could be combined in an infinite number of ways. There were more complex commands and structures that took longer to do, but once done by a magic user, you never had to do them again; you simply called them out in your regular spell casting.

Sean got it immediately: magic was a programming language. Plain and simple, the same basic fundamentals were there, all of them! The logic statements, the branches, the tests, it was all there! Even variables, pointers, names. It was all about building objects and manipulating them! Magic was an object-oriented language!

Digging through the book further, he even found the parallels to serial programming, though he could find nothing on parallel programming. He wondered briefly if *that* thought had ever occurred to anyone? Maybe it was in an advanced text? They mentioned ritual covens with more than one user, so perhaps it was there.

Sean briefly wondered about the underlying structure of the language. Computers had compilers that turned code into machine code, a basic structure of ones and zeros that people used by assigning labels to them and called 'assembly code' to make it easier to remember. He wondered if that existed as well?

Setting that book down, he saw one titled 'Advanced Magical Structures'. Picking that one up, he started in immediately. The book was all about how complicated spells worked, the high-level ones, Sean guessed. Obviously it wasn't a book for a novice like him, because the book described very advanced spells and how they were constructed.

But Sean had almost no problems figuring it out; it was so close to his object-oriented textbook that Sean was shocked by the similarities. Objects, classes, inheritance, polymorphism, data hiding and encapsulation, it was all there. The parallels between it and several other languages were shockingly close, close enough that Sean started to wonder if he could just use one of those languages instead?

But then how would he implement it? Putting the book down, he started to look for an intermediate guide, something that would teach him how to craft spells. Someplace to start. Just because he was pretty sure he understood the theory didn't mean he could actually cast any spells.

That was when he felt something tugging on him, so he quickly found the exit from the 'classroom' and opened his eyes. Both Roxy and Jolene were looking down at him on the bed.

"What time is it?" Sean asked, looking around.

"Dinner time," Roxy said, "you weren't sleeping on me, were you?"

Sean shook his head. Swinging his legs off the bed, he sat there a minute and looked at them.

"No, I was studying the basics; it's fascinating, really!"

"Why's that?"

"It's like computer programming! It's just another programming language, with its own syntax and structures! The theory is all so similar," Sean smiled, "it looks like all of those computer courses I took will still pay off."

"Have you learned how to cast anything?" Jolene asked.

"No, not yet. That was what I was starting on when you interrupted me. Honestly though, now that you mention it, I'm pretty hungry. I had no idea I'd been in there that long."

"Isn't there any kind of a clock?"

"Not that I've noticed."

"Maybe you should try looking at your watch?" Roxy suggested.

Sean shrugged. "Sure, why not? So, what's for dinner?"

"We're gonna hit the buffet tonight," Jolene said, "you're driving."

"Is that safe?" Sean asked.

"We're going to find out." Roxy shrugged.

Jolene nodded. "The buffet is in the Silver Legacy, so it's all under casino security, and it's pretty full on a Wednesday. Plus somebody warded the whole place decades ago."

"Warded?" Sean asked, giving her a curious look.

"Best I can guess is someone with power either liked going to the buffet there or to gamble, so they warded the entire casino against scrying. The only way anyone is going to know you're there is by physically finding you."

"Oh." Sean nodded. "Oh! Do you think you can ward my mom's car? Seeing as we're using it?"

Jolene thought about that a moment. "I think I can keep anyone from realizing it's yours when you're not in it. But they'll still be able to find you if they're trying hard enough."

"How come it worked with the house?"

"Because the house doesn't move." Jolene laughed.

"And why can't you just hide me from them?"

"Not my type of magic. Even the protections I cast on this place aren't in my normal realm, but my old master had learned them, because tantric masters are often unpopular with the rest of the magical community."

"Really?"

Jolene grinned. "Magic users have more essence for us to tap off of than normal humans. So we're very willing to sleep with them, and well," Jolene smirked then, "for some reason their wives or husbands just don't seem to understand."

"Go figure!" Roxy laughed.

"Well, seeing as you're ours now," Sean winked at Jolene, "I don't think they'll be worrying about you much longer."

"Ummm," Jolene squirmed a little, "I think I found you a new place to live," Jolene said, changing the subject.

Roxy and Sean both looked at her questioningly.

"The old Belvedere tower, the taller one."

"Isn't that abandoned still?" Sean asked.

"Yup! And that's exactly why it's a good place. No one lives there, but the smaller tower next door is full of people. So you can lose yourself in the crowd, then go up to the top floor."

"How do we get in? Isn't the place next door a gated building?"

Jolene smiled and nodded. "That's the best part. It's hard to get into without a keycard."

"Which we don't have," Roxy pointed out.

"Now you do." Jolene smiled and gave them each one.

"How did you get these?"

"Simple, I live there." Jolene grinned.

"I thought you lived on campus?" Sean blinked and looked at her. "You're not a student?"

"Oh, I'm a student, but *you* try to bring someone back to your dorm rooms for sex! Yeah, that didn't work out well at all."

Sean realized that the idea of Jolene having sex with other men was not sitting well with him. He coughed when he realized he was starting to growl.

"So, ah," Sean said, noticing the look Roxy gave him, and the confused expression on Jolene's face, "what are you studying?"

"Oh! Physical therapy. It's a good way to get my hands on people and tap into their essence, and because I know a lot of body manipulation spells,

I can actually do something for them. Beyond massaging and stuff, that is."

"You know, I've been wondering, what happens if you drain all of someone's 'essence'?"

"Usually they just fall asleep," Jolene said, "though I suppose I could kill someone if I went beyond that point and tried to drain their actual life force. But I don't know how to do that, and honestly, I'd rather not learn. It's icky."

"Well that's a relief." Sean smiled.

"Eh, I'm not sure I could drain a lycan. You guys have a lot more essence than regular humans."

"Yeah, I noticed I seem to have a lot of magical energy when I was looking at my, well, 'stats' in that magical spreadsheet they use."

"Everything about lycans is magical, Hon," Roxy told him. "I would have thought that to be obvious, I mean we turn into animals and can regenerate damn near anything."

Sean nodded; it *was* obvious, once he considered it.

"Just don't use up *all* of your essence or mana," Jolene warned.

"Why? What happens then?" Sean asked, a little worried.

"Then you'll be stuck in whatever shape you're in until you recover enough to shift."

"You'll also heal slower," Roxy pointed out, "which will leave you more vulnerable to normal attacks."

"Good things to know. Well, let's get going."

Grabbing his things, Sean put on a light vest to make it a little less obvious that he had the massive gun strapped to his side.

When they got to the casino, Sean went up a few floors in the parking garage, where there were fewer cars and fewer places for an ambush to hide, then they all went down and had dinner. For once, Sean felt like he got his money's worth, because he was able to really pack it away.

When they finally left, he had his right arm around Roxy's waist and his left one around Jolene's, holding them close as they walked. Sean noticed he got a few looks from Jolene when he put his arm around her, so he bent over and kissed her, making her blush. He kissed Roxy then, just so she wouldn't feel left out.

"This way," Jolene said and instead of leading them back to their car, she led them out and down the street.

"Okay, there are a few ways to get into the big tower from the smaller one, and I made sure there aren't any cameras on them. I think there are ways in from beneath the street as well."

"Beneath the street?" Sean asked.

"Sewers, water, power, phone," Jolene replied and led them up to the back side of the shorter tower. Using her keycard, she buzzed them in, then took a left, and they went down a long hallway with a few doors off of it.

"Maintenance access; most of the people living here don't know about it, but some of us use it because it's convenient."

Sean and Roxy just nodded. When they came to the end of the hallway, there was a heavy door.

"This is kept locked, but they keep the key right here," Jolene said as she bent down and ran her hand along the underside of a small metal box.

"The key is magnetic, and there's a magnet in the box. So someone I guess decided to stick it there."

"Is that someone you?" Roxy giggled.

"Um, could be?" Jolene giggled back and unlocked the door, then replaced the key.

Opening the door, they stepped inside, and as Jolene locked it behind them, Sean looked around. They were in the back of a lobby that looked a little dated. It was completely empty and rather dark as the windows and doors were all boarded up. Except for a lone 'Exit' sign above the door they'd just entered that was still lit, there was no other illumination at all.

"Come on, we need to take the stairs. There's no power in here at all."

Sean nodded, and he and Roxy followed Jolene over to a nice wooden door, which, once opened, revealed a stairwell that went down as well as rose all the way up into the darkness.

"How many floors is it?" Roxy asked.

"Twenty."

Sean could see Roxy take off her shoes and push her pants down really low. Then she shifted and smiled at him, tail curling behind her cute butt.

Sean took off the vest, unbuttoned his shirt, kicked off his shoes. Pushing his pants down as well, he shifted too.

Sean had been worried about his pants falling down; they were pretty low on him now, but with his much larger size, they weren't about to go anywhere, especially since the once loose legs were now nice and snug.

"Here, hold these," Sean said to Jolene after picking up his shoes and handed them to Jolene along with his vest.

"You expect me to carry this all the way up for you?" Jolene said, scowling at him.

Sean squatted down in front of her. "Hop on."

"Oh!" Jolene said and quickly got on Sean's back.

"I didn't think you wanted to climb forty flights of stairs." Sean chuckled and followed Roxy as she started up the stairs quickly.

"So, what's on the floors we're passing?" Roxy asked softly as they climbed.

"Condos," Jolene said. "They were rebuilding this place when the economy crashed. So they just abandoned it for now."

"You've looked at them?" Sean asked.

"Some. Mostly they're just walls and fittings for fixtures. Only the first few floors are done."

"Have you been to the top?"

Jolene sighed and nodded. "Yeah, took me almost twenty minutes! I hate going up stairs."

"But you're fine with going down, right?" Sean teased.

"Hey!" Jolene grumbled at him and bit his ear.

"Oooo, do that again!" Sean said and slowed down a moment, purring loudly.

"What'd you do, Jolene?" Roxy asked, looking back at the two of them.

"I bit his ear! Isn't the supposed to hurt?"

Roxy laughed. "It's a form of foreplay. For us big cats, that is! Now, if you want to play, how about you wait until we get to the top?"

"Yes, the toooop!" Sean purred, grinning, as Jolene just sighed

When they got to the top, they exited the stairwell through the fire door onto the penthouse floor. It was actually rather nice!

"What the hell? Why is this finished?" Roxy asked.

"They never gutted the penthouse in the remodel," Jolene told her as she slid off Sean's back. "Everything is in here; beds, chairs, tables, bathrooms, showers, the whole lot. Best of all?" Jolene grinned. "The power may be off, but the water is still on."

"The water's on? Why?" Sean asked, looking around. There were plastic tarps over all the tables and couches. Looking into one of the rooms, there was a nice big bed, also with a tarp over it.

"Water sprinklers. They have to keep the lines charged, and well, they turned off the other floors when they stripped them out for the remodel, but as they never got to this one, they never turned it off."

Nodding, Sean smiled and started to pull off his shirt as well as his holster, set them down on the floor, then very carefully peeled his pants off.

"What are you doing?" Jolene asked.

"Both of you!" Sean grinned, and reaching out, snagged Jolene's hand before she could move out of reach.

"What?" Jolene said, but she was grinning.

"Well, don't you have to protect this place or something?" Sean purred and, walking over to the large bed, he pulled the plastic drop cloth off with his free hand as he pulled Jolene along with the other.

"Going to join us, Dear?" Sean asked, smiling at Roxy, who had also shed her clothes.

"Wouldn't miss it for the world," Roxy purred.

"You know I don't need to have sex to put my protections down, right?" Jolene giggled.

"I just want to make sure you do it *right*, is all," Sean purred.

Jolene laughed, then looked shocked as Sean kissed her, still in his hybrid form. This was something she hadn't expected!

"Aren't you going to shift?" Jolene asked him, looking up and down at the size of him; she'd slept with some fairly large men, but none had been as big as Sean now was.

"I thought you were supposed to be kinky?" Sean teased.

"You weigh enough to crush me!"

"Don't worry, you can be on top!" Sean grinned, lying down on the bed.

"I'm not going to get a choice on this, am I?"

"I warned you!" Roxy said, pushing Jolene from behind onto the bed with Sean.

"Warned her, what?" Sean asked, looking up at the two of them as he spread out on his back.

"That sooner or later, if she didn't run while she had the chance, she was gonna end up in your pride!" Roxy giggled.

"Oh, guess she wants it then," Sean purred.

"And why do you say *that*?" Jolene chuckled.

"Because not only didn't you run, but you're taking your clothes off."

Jolene blushed fiercely. Yeah, she wanted him alright. Roxy too. They were both brimming with power; with them she really wouldn't need anyone else! And honestly? Anyone who claimed that 'variety is the spice of life' never had a favorite restaurant. She already had an emotional attachment to Roxy, and damned if she wasn't forming one to Sean already. Otherwise, she wouldn't have spent seven hours searching the city today for a place for him to hole up.

"Um, let's just say that your offer brings a lot to the table and I'm...eep!"

Sean dragged her down and kissed her. "I love you Jolene, and you love both of us. Now, how about we make some magic?"

Roxy groaned at the corny line as Sean smiled.

Jolene sighed, but smiled as well.

"Yes, let's."

Thursday - Moving Day

Sean looked at his backpack; he'd gotten several pairs of pants and half of his shirts into it, along with quite a few of his shoes. All the rest of his clothing, except for one set, he'd stuffed in his duffel bag, which he'd leave in the trunk of the car.

His laptop had gone into his backpack; he'd decided he'd try to finish out the courses of the three professors who'd agreed to let him finish up remotely. All his other courses he'd dropped.

He'd also grabbed a couple of textbooks he thought might help him.

Then he'd looked around the room for anything important that he just had to take with him. Sadly, there wasn't a single thing. He'd gotten the folded box out from under his bed, tossed everything else of that was left, which other than books, his pillow, and his bed sheets, amounted to a plastic Vault-Boy statue, and an old Final Fantasy Eleven clock.

"One of these days," Sean sighed, "I'm going to own some actual stuff."

Picking up the box, he took it to Roxy's room.

"Are you sure it's alright to leave this here?" he asked her.

"Sure, Hon. Not like I'm going to be here much anymore, myself." Roxy shrugged. She hadn't told him yet, but she'd already dropped two of her classes, as well as told the track team coach she was dealing with family issues and wouldn't be at anymore meets this semester.

Thankfully the coach had been sympathetic instead of a pain and had already leaned on her instructors to 'go easy on her' so she wouldn't lose her scholarship. Seeing as she was already a good student with good grades, Roxy suspected she'd get passing marks in the rest of her classes even if she didn't show up for the rest of the year.

"When are you telling the landlord you're moving out?" Roxy asked Sean.

"I already sent him an email telling him I wouldn't be here after Saturday," Sean said and shrugged. "What about your room?"

"My dad pays for it; if we decide we can't come back here, he'll just hire someone to come in here, pack it all up, and have it shipped home."

Sean nodded. "Let me get my stuff, and we'll get out of here."

Going back to his room, Sean picked up his backpack and his duffel bag, and looked around the room. He'd miss it; he'd lived here almost two years now. His first time on his own. It was nice, it was cheap, and it was within walking distance to everything. But it wasn't safe anymore. Sooner or later, they'd stop trying to find him with magic, and they'd resort to more mundane means.

He had to be ready for that. The last thing he wanted to do was subject the others living here to the kinds of people who were after him.

Walking out and closing the door behind him, he went back to Roxy's room. After putting his backpack on, he picked up her duffel bag as well as his, and they went down to his car.

"Moving out?" George, the other guy living on the top floor, asked him.

"Yeah, my neighbor died and left me his house," Sean sighed, "I figured it would be cheaper to live there, even with the commute."

"Wow, I don't know if I should offer condolences or congratulations," George said. "Are you going with him too?" he asked Roxy.

"After the semester ends." She smiled. "Enjoy the break!"

"Definitely! You two have fun!" George said and went back into his room.

"How long before everyone hears about that?" Roxy snickered as they walked down the stairs.

"Hopefully long before people start coming around here looking for me," Sean replied.

Going outside to the car, Sean tossed everything into the trunk, then gave Roxy a kiss.

"I'll see you later tonight," Roxy told him, "after I finish classes."

"Keep your eyes open, and be careful," Sean warned her.

"Don't worry. It's you they want, and I doubt they even know about me."

"Yet," Sean said.

"Yet," Roxy agreed and nodded.

Kissing her again, he got into the car, and with a wave he drove off. Everything seemed still outside, almost oppressive. Like a massive storm was building, and he wanted to be back inside before whatever was coming let go. Nobody had tried anything in days, and his birthday was only a week away. Sean figured if they'd been desperate before, they'd be getting even worse over the next few days.

"Just how safe is this place?" Sean asked Jolene as he looked out the window again over the city. There *was* a storm brewing, you could see it, and everything about it felt wrong.

"With the amount of magic I dumped into it last night?" Jolene came up behind him and gave Sean a hug. "I don't think you've got anything to worry about."

"Something about that storm isn't right," Sean said, unconsciously moving back from the window as the sky got darker.

Sean's cell phone rang; opening it, he looked at the number; it was Roxy.

"What's wrong?" Sean asked immediately.

"Someone set the apartment house on fire." Roxy was panting, hard, and there was a lot of wind noise.

"What? Where are you?" Sean demanded.

"I'm running through the streets about as fast as I can. There were people outside, waiting. They didn't stop me or anyone else as we ran out. As soon as I got out of sight I shifted, and I think I hit a personal best on my speed for a few minutes there."

"I'll come get you," Sean growled.

"No, this storm doesn't feel right. Stay there. I'm almost there, anyway."

"Okay," Sean growled and hung up the phone, then looked at Jolene, who was looking a little pale. "Did you hear that?"

"I think I better redouble my wards," Jolene said a bit worriedly, and immediately set to work doing just that.

His phone rang again; it was Detective Schumer.

"Yes, Detective?" Sean asked a little nervously.

"You okay, Sean? You sound worried."

"Someone just set my apartment house on fire. Yeah, I'm a little nervous. Why are you calling?"

"Well, I'm afraid I have some more bad news for you," Detective Schumer started.

"Oh god, please don't tell me my mother's dead!"

"No, it's not your mother, Sean."

Sean sighed. "Thank god."

"Your house blew up. So did Sampson's."

"What?" Sean asked, shocked.

"They blew up. Together. About an hour ago. My boss called the sheriff, and he's got the State Police over there right now; they've got their boys on it. We've got the city's bomb people checking it out as well, and I think even the BATF might be getting involved."

"Shit," Sean swore, "was anybody hurt?"

"Thankfully, no. Whoever blew them up put the bombs underneath and used shaped charges. At least that's what the bomb squad is telling me. It just blew everything straight up, and set whatever was left on fire."

"I was just over there yesterday." Sean gulped. "I was thinking of moving back to keep an eye on things until my mother got home."

Sean looked around and found a couch to sit down on.

"Just what the hell are you involved in, Son?"

"I think the people who murdered my father have decided they want me dead now too." Sean sighed.

"Your father's death was an accident, Sean. I've seen the report."

"Yeah, well, then why the hell are people trying to kill me? Why is my mom missing? Why is Sampson dead, and what the hell were those people doing in our homes?"

"Maybe you should come down to the station house, Sean. We can protect you."

"Sorry, but I'm not sure I like the idea of being someplace where just anybody can find me right now. Don't call me, I'll call you."

Sean hung up the phone, shut it off, and then to be extra safe, he took the battery out of it.

"Come on," Jolene said, running up and grabbing his arm, "we need to move."

"What? I thought you said it was safe here?"

"From wizards, warlocks, mages, and the rest, yeah. But that's not what's looking for you right now, and we need to get underground, *fast!*"

"What about Roxy?"

"Well grab her on the way down; now move it, Sean!"

Sean shifted into his hybrid form and ignored the two buttons that flew off his shirt. Sticking his phone and the battery in his pocket, he scooped up Jolene, threw her over his shoulder, and made for the fire door at a run as he heard the first crack of lightning. It sounded close, too close.

Running down the stairs four or five steps at a time, he rounded a corner about ten flights down and narrowly avoided crashing into Roxy, who was heading up.

"Follow!" he yelled and continued down, taking the stairwell past the lobby floor and down into the basement.

"Look for the water mains, we can hide behind them!" Jolene said.

Sean started searching the basement, which seemed to be mostly storage now.

"What are we hiding from?" Roxy asked.

"Lightning elementals. That storm isn't natural."

"Well, yeah, I guessed that! But what does that have to do with lightning?

"Lightning elementals need a storm to survive in our world. That's why the storm was created, so they could summon the elementals and send them to kill Sean."

"They can do that?" Roxy said, horrified.

"Not easily; this is a major piece of magic. It had to have taken at least twenty people working together, and they probably spent all day yesterday preparing, then all day today casting."

Sean kicked in a locked door marked 'Fire Riser Room' and, sure enough, the water mains were inside. Running back over to the girls, he grabbed them and started pulling them there.

"How do you know so much about regular magic? I thought tantric magic was different?" Roxy asked Jolene.

"Magic is magic; the differences between me and them is their power is more innate. I sacrificed my innate power when I became a tantric mage."

"Why would you do a thing like that?" Sean asked as they got down under the pipes, which ran about four feet off the ground, branching off an eighteen-inch-wide main that came up from the level below.

"Because I can hold a lot more power than they can, so I don't have to depend on magical items or other people."

"You just have to fuck a lot," Sean pointed out.

"Yeah, well, I like sex, and I haven't heard any complaints from you!" Jolene smirked. "But, yeah, it's always good to know what the other folks can do. There aren't enough of the higher-level folks in any one coven or council in this town to do this. They had to band several of them together."

"You're sure of that?" Roxy asked.

"Of course I'm sure." she grinned suddenly. "I called Sawyer the moment I noticed something while strengthening the wards. He told me to go to ground and to warn everyone I know."

"Why's that?" Roxy gave Jolene a concerned look.

"Because if you go to all this trouble to raise a bunch of lightning elementals, you're not just going to waste it on one target. You better believe they made promises to clean up some 'other issues' in order to make this work."

"So," Sean asked, "does a lightning elemental look like a ball of static electricity?"

"Huh?"

Sean pointed out the doorway and into the area they'd just left. There, coming down the staircase, was what could only be described as a ball of lighting.

"Shit," Jolene said. Pulling out a piece of chalk, she started drawing on the floor. "Guys, I know this is rude, but if the two of you could start fucking like bunnies, that would be great."

"What?" Sean said, blinking.

"I gotta work fast, or that thing might kill one of us. Now, get to work!"

Roxy gave a strangled laugh and, grabbing her shorts, she used her claws to rip them off, coming over to straddle Sean's lap.

"Umm, talk about your pressure!" Sean gulped, pushing his own pants down further and exposing his crotch.

"Oh, don't worry, Sean, I bet I can get you excited," Roxy purred and started to rub her crotch over his.

Sean turned and focused on Roxy, his sexy Roxy, and tried to ignore the crackling death that was slowly coming closer as Jolene started drawing lines and circles like a demented street artist.

"I suggest you hurry!" Jolene called over her shoulder. "It hasn't sensed us yet, but once it does..."

Roxy smiled and leaned in, kissing him slowly, warmly, as she purred. Breaking the kiss, she then put her lips to her ears and whispered softly, so only he could hear, "How about putting some cubs in my belly, hmmm? Would my big strong lion like to breed his sexy little cheetah?"

Sean gasped as his lion literally *surged* into his consciousness with a very positive and strong reaction. Suddenly he was hard as a rock, and Roxy was working her way back down onto his lap, driving him up inside her.

"Cubs!" he growled, the idea had never once occurred to him, but apparently this was something very basic to his lion psyche.

"Oh yeah," Roxy whispered, "when this is over, we're going to make lots of cubs, you and me!"

Sean really couldn't help himself, he grabbed her hips and went to work.

"Good!" Jolene called. "Take my hand, Roxy; I need a conduit for the power."

Sean was barely aware of anything beyond Roxy at this point. She was smiling at him, and kissing him, and of course moving up and down on him, driving him onward. It didn't matter to him that they were in a cold dark dank dirty basement, sitting on a floor under a bunch of pipes. The woman he loved had just unleashed a promise unlike any other, and his lion was enthralled with the idea, which meant he was enthralled with it, too.

Sean didn't even notice the thin misty wall that suddenly formed around them going from the floor to the pipes just as the elemental came into the room. The moment it saw them it surged forward, but hitting the thin wall, it screamed like an electric motor spinning at its limit. Sean only paid it half a mind as he was already at his peak, and pulling Roxy down hard, he shuddered through his orgasm, surprised that Roxy joined him though he'd been rather quick this time. She collapsed against him, panting as hard as he was.

"Is it dead?" Roxy asked, panting as the scream slowly subsided to a whine, then stopped altogether.

"It is now." Jolene sighed and, falling back to sit on her butt, she blew out a breath and wiped the back of her hand across her forehead. "Thanks guys, I couldn't have done that without you."

"Does this mean they know we're here?" Sean asked, panting hard.

"No, they've got so many of these things running around, they won't know who they've killed until after the elementals do it and return. I suspect this guy won't be the only one missing; it's not like these things have a lot of smarts."

Sean nodded.

"But I think it would be for the best if we stayed down here for a while. Like say, until sunrise?"

Sean nodded again then, giving Roxy a hug, he put a finger under her chin and tipped it up so he could kiss her.

"You know I'm going to hold you to that promise?" he whispered.

"You better!" Roxy mock-growled. "A girl makes a promise like that to her man and she sure as hell expects him to hold her to it!"

"What promise was that?" Jolene asked, absently.

"Children, she promised me children," Sean purred, then turned to look at Jolene, who looked rather shocked.

"What?"

Sean smirked. "Don't worry, your turn will come."

"Thank god lycans and humans can't breed." Jolene sighed.

"Thank god I can just bite you and fix that!" Sean growled at Jolene with a wink.

"You know, I think I liked it better when I was afraid of being electrocuted."

Friday - After the Storm

"So, what did you learn?" Sean asked Jolene as he looked out the window across the city. The three of them had spent the day in one of the innermost rooms, doing not much more than sleeping, cuddling, and talking. After they'd 'topped off' Jolene's magical reserves, of course.

"Well, Sawyer knows of ten dead so far. Three were magic users from a small coven that one of the groups involved in raising the storm yesterday had issues with, two were the surviving Lithos who were in the hospital recovering from their wounds. Apparently a lightning bolt surged into the room during the storm, and as they were shackled to their stretchers, they got electrocuted.

"Another three were lycan leaders who've been stirring up dissent against the mages; Sawyer thinks this was a show of strength to cut down on any rumors of your father's work suddenly freeing them. One was the ex-wife of one of the mages who leads the Totis Viribus council. Evidently she divorced him and was taking him to the cleaners."

"Mages get divorced?" Roxy laughed. "I thought they were too jealous of their powers to even get married?"

"She was a dancer in one of the bigger shows, quite the looker, I gather. Apparently his promises of fame and fortune didn't pan out or something. According to Sawyer, she said he was lousy in bed and was sharing that opinion far and wide. I think it was that more than the money that got her killed." Jolene sighed.

"Who was the last one?"

"No idea, Sawyer didn't recognize the name, he thinks it was just some poor bastard who was in the wrong place at the wrong time, and an elemental decided to kill him anyway. They're not the easiest to control."

"So how long before we go through this again?" Sean asked.

"Hard to say. Sawyer also heard two of the casters dropped dead after they ended the circle. Apparently not killing you led to some sort of feedback or squabble within the group, or maybe the elemental major they'd promised your power to decided to take theirs instead." Jolene shrugged. "That's another problem with summoning extra-planer beings. Sometimes they kill you."

"Well," Sean said, turning to look at Jolene and Roxy, "we might as well clean up, go out, and hit the buffet. I'm starving, and I'm sure the rest of you are too. Hopefully after what just happened, all anyone wants to do is spend a few days recovering."

"Your birthday is in a week, Sean; I'm not so sure they're going to be doing all that much resting." Roxy sighed.

"And there are still a lot of other groups out there," Jolene agreed. "But that storm stirred up so much shit nobody's going to be scrying for anyone in this town for at least another twelve hours."

Sean nodded. "Oh, that reminds me," he said and fished the key for Sampson's tool shed out of his pocket. "Ever seen a key like this?"

Jolene took it and looked at it a moment. "If I had to guess, and I don't because I'm a magic user chock full of power, I'd say it opens a safety deposit box down at the Heritage Bank."

"That's my bank!" Sean said, surprised.

"The South Town Crossing branch," she added.

"Why all the way down there?" Sean wondered.

"Who cares?" Roxy sighed and got up. "I hate cold showers, but I'm starving! Let's go eat, then we can hit the bank."

"It's after six." Sean sighed. "They're closed.

"Well, we can go tomorrow then."

"They're closed weekends too." Sean said and shook his head.

"Well, shit!" Roxy swore. "Shower, food, and then, well, I don't know! More food!" She stomped off towards the bathroom.

"Is it just me, or has it been a rough week?" Sean sighed, shaking his head.

Jolene laughed. "Seven days ago you were human, without a care in the world. Yeah, I'd say it's been a rough week."

"Well, let's go join her, I'm starving, too."

"You know, the water in my shower is heated, and it's not that far of a walk from here."

"Oh, well. Should we tell her before or after she jumps into a freezing cold shower?" Sean grinned.

"I heard that!" Roxy yelled from the next room.

It was late, just after three in the morning. Sean had spent the last three hours studying magic. There was a whole school devoted to protecting one's self from scrying, from spying, from being detected by other casters. A lot of it was pretty simple, so he'd decided to make that his first avenue of study.

He understood the language, and he thought he understood the methods it employed. The problem, as always, was in the practice. Learning how to execute the spell, to manipulate the magic forces so you could execute your program. That was the hard part, and that was the part that would need the most training to learn.

He had found in the books on the desk a very thin one labeled 'Learning to Cast'. It had five very simple spells with detailed instructions on how to cast each one. It was supposed to be the first step for every magic user, so he'd gone over it and reread the instructions on the first spell more than a dozen times. All he needed now was to try and cast it.

Well, there was no time like the present.

Getting out of bed, he looked down at Roxy and Jolene, who were curled together happily. Jolene had opted to spend the night with them, rather than return to her own bed. Her loyalties were quickly becoming clear; it was obvious he had another female in his pride. It was just a matter of time until she admitted it.

He could feel his lion was rather proud about that.

'I think she loves Roxy as much as she loves us,' he told his lion.

'All the better; you want your wives to be happy with each other, too, don't you?'

Sean thought he detected a faint smirk there.

Standing in the center of the room and closing his eyes, Sean started on his first practice spell, lighting a candle. He'd substituted a piece of string sitting on an upturned glass; hopefully the spell wouldn't mind.

Clearing his mind, he ran the spell through it, focused on the string.

Nothing happened.

He tried again, and again nothing happened. He tried it a hundred times, and it failed a hundred.

Going back into his classroom, he reread the instructions in the book; reread the notes and the suggestions. All to try and get an idea of what he might be doing wrong.

Then he tried again, and again and again. He cursed at it, swore at it, threatened it, replaced the glass with a new one after he smacked it across the room and broke it.

By the time the sun came through the windows, he was dead tired, and his mind was almost numb.

"Ah fuck it, I need to sleep." He sighed and waved his hand at it, casting one last time.

His roar of success brought both girls running.

"Finally!" Sean crowed as he watched the small flame quickly consuming the piece of thread. "Success!"

"Do it again," Jolene told him.

"What? I'm going to bed."

"No you're not!" she told him and, plucking a hair off of her head, she held it in front of him.

"Do it again, now!"

Sighing, Sean took a moment, and casting again, the piece of hair lit on fire.

"Find something we can rip up to burn," Jolene said to Roxy, and dropping the piece of hair, she plucked out another one.

"Again!"

"Come on, Jolene, I'm tired!"

"You can go to sleep after you've done it fifty times, Sean! This is important, now quit yer whining, and do it!"

Sean grumbled, but he did it again. By that point Roxy had returned with a dollar bill and was using her claws to slice off thin strips.

"Again!"

"Do we have to?" Sean grumbled, but did as he was told.

"Yes." Jolene smiled as the piece she was holding lit on fire. Dropping it, she stepped on it and took another one from Roxy.

"Why?"

"So when you wake up, you haven't forgotten. Now, again!"

Sean nodded and resigned himself to doing it over and over. Until eventually Jolene said he was finished and could go get some sleep.

"Congratulations, Hon," Jolene said as he turned to head off to bed. Coming over to him, she kissed him. "You're now a magic user."

Sean yawned and nodded, looking at all the little burnt scraps on the floor.

Then he smiled the same way Roxy had that night on the bus.

"Now I just need to figure out how to make all of those bastards pay!"

End Book One

Afterword

Hi! I'd like to thank you for reading my story Black Friday, I hope you enjoyed it, and if you did I would greatly appreciate it if you would rate and review it on Amazon. We do get rewarded by Amazon, when we get four and five star reviews, and of course, the more we get, the more we get rewarded.

What is that reward you ask? Simple: Amazon will show my book to people who they think will enjoy it, like you did.

So please! I'd appreciate it very much if you gave me a good review.

If you'd like to read more about the continuing trials of Sean, Roxy, and Jolene, as he tries to find his way through this new world he's been dropped into the middle of while trying to continue his father's work, please buy the next book in the series when it comes out!

Update: Currently, book nine is nearing release, with several more planned. The story has been split into three arcs, of approximately six books each. The first arc has been completed, and the second arc is well underway. I've updated this afterword since hiring an editor to help go over the books. Any remaining errors are mine; don't be afraid to write if you find any.

(Later books in this series have not yet been titled, though the plots have been developed)

Other stories of mine already out: Shadow, which can be found, along with this on Amazon, by going to my Amazon Author's webpage at:

https://www.amazon.com/Jan-Stryvant/e/B06ZY7L62L/

Or my *own* webpage at:
www.vanstry.net/stryvant/

Occasional announcements at:
https://stryvant.blogspot.com/

Made in the USA
San Bernardino, CA
03 November 2019

59385305R00124